W0007050

TABLE OF CONTENTS

ACKNOWLEDGMENTS

For Connie, Jason, Emily, Barbara, Jakob and Luke.

To all my family members in Canada and the U.K. For wonderful cherished friends everywhere, fun times and fond memories. Heart-felt thanks for your encouragement, patience and support.

With a special shout-out to my sister Maureen ❤

This book is dedicated to my Uncle George, recalling those bygone days at number 55.

In appreciation of the inspiration, always lively conversation and entertainment enhanced by Frank, Ella, movie talk, cocktails, and Passing Clouds.

Together from
The beginning
David
xo

THE TELEPORTER'S HANDBOOK

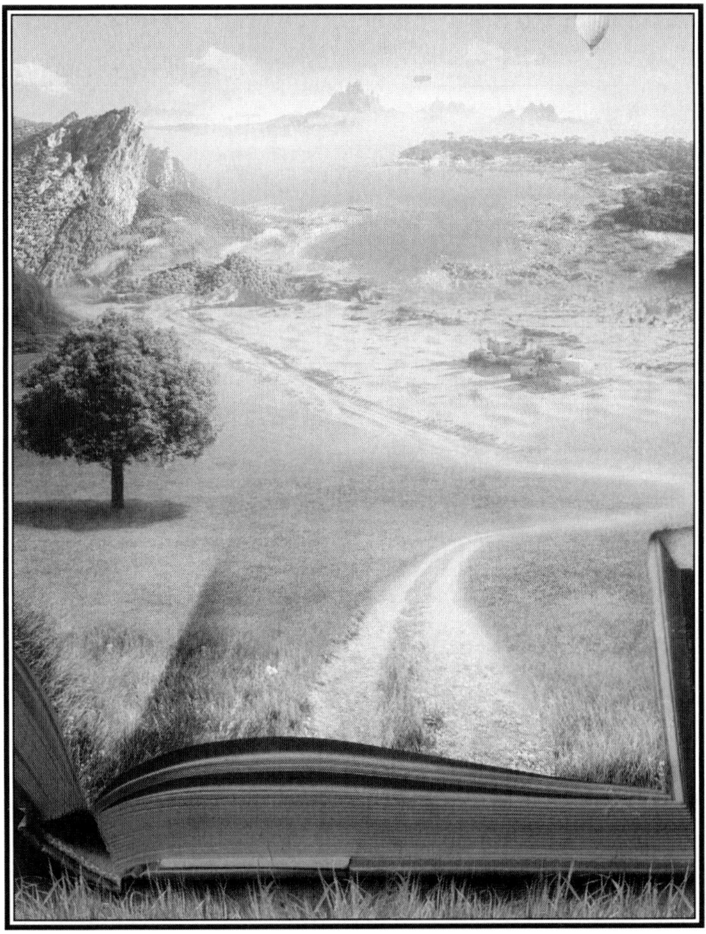

Notes from The Front (1)

UBO Base. Zone 3. A deserted village in the Ukraine. The streets are empty. Dust clouds full of carcinogens billow and swirl down the deserted crossroads. The doors of houses without hinges and the few windows intact are not inviting you in. On the corner of a once busy boulevard, an abandoned café with tables and chairs overturned. The espresso machine that once transformed beans into lattes, mochas, and cappuccinos, is smashed beyond repair. A small, brightly coloured poster left pinned to a board on the wall announces:

Next Wednesday October 23. A meeting of the UBO (Ugly Babies Org.) will take place here. Adopting new recruits to help in delivering food and water to the war zone refugees. We are gathering strength and fully committed to saving the planet before it is destroyed. Join us! Free refreshments and pastries will be served.

The promise of this better world is painted in bold brush strokes of positive encouragement. It may have come too late. But we should start our story closer to the beginning.

Trafalgar House Terrace, London, S.W.1

Bernard Talbot poured a second cup of coffee and deliberated over the article he had just read. The question asked was, 'How many gentle flowers grow in an English Country Garden?' And according to page three of The Sentinel, Priscilla Talbot was not one them. Although Bernard considered the photo of his sister a reasonable likeness, it was not flattering. Bernard knew how these profile articles could position you in public opinion with one snapshot. He was a controversial archaeologist, noted for his published works on the arrival of Beaker People (c. 2900 –1800 BC). That period witnessed weapons and artifacts made from stone and bone being replaced by the use of copper and gold. Welcome to the Bronze Age. Or, as Priscilla coined it, "The Birth of Bling!" Ten years younger than himself, she was at thirty-one continually upsetting the status quo. The featured article headline read, "Renowned Scientific Anthropologist, Priscilla Talbot. Doomsday Kook or Visionary Futurist?" Most of the statements attributed to Priscilla were to provoke the proponents of late liberalism. Those old school power mongers who had controlled and governed while busy lining their own pockets. That model of bio politics, having served them for so long, was now a slippery fish they were holding only by the tail fin. Priscilla was further quoted stating, "Current capitalism leaves too many people wandering impoverished in the wilderness." And, "Their experiment of multiculturalism had failed." She was proposing a new frontier and a model based on digitally savvy kids getting into a relationship with their own innovative ideas to generate income. Further claiming, there were new universal spiritual and scientific paths to follow beyond a specific culture. Bernard could feel the heat of the impending backlash. Dear Priscilla, a child prodigy, was always prone and still apparently, playing with fire. Entering university, she had risen quickly in academic circles, immediately accepted among her peers and mentors. A super nova discovered, recognized and celebrated. Tributes and offers showered like wedding confetti, would have quickly submerged her, but for the fact Priscilla had a mind of her own. And instead of taking the path lined with rose petals and applause, she chose a less established and a more contentious alternative route. And that was one thing you could always count on; Priscilla challenged domineering sovereignty in preference of demanding justice for the underdog. Trying to describe Priscilla in simple terms to those who did not know her was tricky. Innovative genius? True. But shit disturber was equally appropriate. Bernard sent out a silent thought message to her.

"Hey Buttons, Brother Bernie saying hello. Try to stay out of trouble. I'm busy dodging bullets with your name on them. Here as always whenever you need me."

Bernard was her guardian angel, watchdog and protector. Providing a shield deflecting barbed comments, twitter and texts, acting as a positive spokesperson on her behalf. Handling the deluge of derogatory questions such as; "Who on earth does she think she is. Does any sane person endorse or support what she is proposing? Why did she ever leave Mars? When is she going back?" And so on. Thereby confirming a motto Priscilla lived by.

"Life perpetuates questions looking for answers."

Bernard knew no one really cared about the who, where, when and why. The only important question to answer was… "What happens next?" He carefully cut out the picture and article from the newspaper to be pasted into the growing Priscilla scrapbook. This latest article carried a note of serious concern for him. Leaving him to contemplate a new battalion of thoughts circling in the dark.

The First Experiment: Talbot Residence, Windstone, 2019

This was it. The moment all the work it took to get here was going to deliver or fail.

Priscilla was upstairs in the bedroom of the house where she had grown up as a child. She was about to test the first of two experiments. Either of which, if successful, would harness the untethered speculation of science fiction into proven scientific fact.

Staring into the full-length mirror, Priscilla focused her mind's eye with the intention to transpose her reflection. She visualized the five points of a star and transmitted each of those points with her intention. Channelling the energy required she dispatched it to the chosen target. A triangular beam engulfed her reflection before rearranging the molecules of the mirror image. Priscilla blinked, and when she looked back into the mirror she saw only the bed, table, desk and furniture and shelves but, not her body. Nothing else about her immediate environment had changed, except Priscilla herself. She moved cautiously at first but discovered she was still able to pick up items and put them down. Taking a book from the shelf she read a paragraph or two just to make sure the words still made sense. Brambles, her beloved cat, purred as usual, responding to her voice and nuzzling her. Yowza! What words could describe what just happened? Priscilla had cracked the motherlode for invisibility. Allowing the person 'cloaked' to observe, research and participate, where that had never been possible before. This significant breakthrough would certainly be useful in combating the oppressors and their destructive regimes. However, the potential for invisibility was going to take some getting used to. Her stomach grumbled in interruption. Priscilla walked downstairs to the kitchen, opened the refrigerator for eggs and began making an omelette. Savouring that moment to reflect on her long journey and the first experiment. She was tired but feeling elated. She decided to tackle the second experiment after a good night's sleep. The undertaking of teleportation. Breaking down the atoms and molecules of a chosen object and moving them through space without physical assistance. If realized, she could be confident of having found a way of loosening the vice grip of the ruthless power brokers stifling so many people and their cultures, in tandem with destroying the ecological balance of the planet. Without question, she would need the help and continued support of her loyal friends. She had known Naomi and Cleo for some time. First meeting as students, making travel plans together, then as young adults attending seminars and music concerts. They had all played a part in bringing her to this point along with the help of the book. The book Cleo had picked up for her in London. The book that had first spoken to her in a dream.

"There is a voice that doesn't use words. Listen."

"What will it reveal?" Priscilla had asked.

"A truth that cannot be tamed," the book answered.

And that was it. The dream ended and was temporarily stored in the back of her mind. That was typical of Priscilla, always jumping ahead of herself. So, in retracing the steps it had taken her to get here. What were they? Okay. There was her adventure trip of self-discovery to Indonesia. The hillside temple in Bali. That was where it had started. Understanding it might be possible to communicate without technology or wires. The book in the dream came later. And certainly, before this power to become invisible. Before today happened, as she recalled it, Priscilla in an earlier trial, had decided to try and contact Naomi by "mind-radio". Just to see if telekinesis would work. Yes, that was how she got here. Ah!! Good. Almost ready. Priscilla flipped the omelette. She was *so* hungry. Hmmm. It looked delicious To anyone watching it would have appeared that a golden omelette, lifted by a spatula, was floating by itself, onto a waiting plate.

Telekinesis: "How About a Nice Cup of Tea?"

Naomi was cleaning up after a stray neighbourhood cat that had wandered into her Aunt Mimi's house and crapped on the shag rug. "Fame and fortune," she thought. "If this is how you end up, who would want to be an actress?"

Disinfecting the rug for the second time that day, Naomi had been summoned to look after her Aunt Mimi, who, to put it bluntly, was losing her marbles. Mimi Chance was recognized in her day as a "promising" screen star. Now, much older, she took to wandering in and out of the many rooms in the house re-enacting some of the roles she had played. Unfortunately, two days ago she latched on to Helga Brunt, from the television series *SwaZtika*. Helga, being a despicable matron of the Third Reich who hated anyone prettier than her, which quite truthfully was almost everybody on the planet. Naomi watched as Aunt Mimi goose stepped in her orange slippers from one room to the next demanding to know who had allowed the small army of cats to invade her privacy. Naomi did her best to explain that the cats were all strays and that it might help if Aunt Mimi didn't open cans of sardines and leave them in various rooms as invitations. Citing her insolence, "Helga" threatened her with starvation, together with hourly electroshock treatments, until she confessed. Naomi, tired of all this unnecessary drama, finally capitulated under pressure rather than sticking a fork in Helga's eye. And, if for no other reason than she couldn't deal with the Third Reich and cat droppings simultaneously, Naomi, passed the buck, without considering the consequences.

"It might have been Mrs. Farrow next door. Though, I cannot be certain."

This propelled an enraged Aunt Mimi out of the house, into the garden and to lift a heavy stone gnome ornament above her head. She hurled it through Mrs. Farrow's patio doors. After shattering glass everywhere, Aunt Mimi began sucking her thumb and protesting her innocence. Mrs. Farrow, normally a decent being, felt threatened and called the police. The police made note of an explanation from Naomi on Mimi's condition. After first collecting autographs from Mimi, followed by a stern warning, they departed. Shortly after this, Aunt Mimi located a stashed bottle of Stolichnaya vodka and was now thankfully, snoring noisily upstairs, rendering Helga mute and harmless, at least for the time being. Naomi was frazzled. Was it worth going through all this for the promise of a future inheritance and free rent? She was supposed to be helping to save the planet for fecks sake but was confined to the claustrophobic attic room with storage boxes. Naomi was tough enough to handle most situations but looking after Aunt Mimi, cleaning up the cat pee and poop and removing the smell of sardines in every room, was more than she could handle. Then and there Naomi accepted suspending becoming a healthier person and decided to resume chain smoking. Now; where did Aunt Mimi keep her Dunhill's? And who can say which character Aunt Mimi might present when she woke up? Heaven help me, if it is Helen Fenchurch, her aunt's acclaimed role as the vicious housekeeper in *The Servant's Revenge*, Naomi thought. A gripping television series by all accounts but not an experience Naomi was looking for in real life. She needed to contact Priscilla. She would know what to do. Naomi was about to do that when she heard the familiar voice. It was Priscilla.

"Hi, Toots, you wanted to talk to me?"

"Priscilla! How did you know I was about to call?

"I'm practicing ancient native skills. Instinctual telepathy. Standard practice among the kahuna priests of Hawaii. Also, many other native cultures all over the world. You sound panicked."

"It's Aunt Mimi."

"Causing problems?"

"Putting it mildly. Yes. What are you up to?"

"Naomi, much to tell you. I'm at home. Meditating and working on developing these new skills. Telekinesis. Telepathic sympatico. I sensed you wanted to talk to me. How is the reception?"

"Timing is perfect. There's a bit of an echo."

"Hmmm. Early exercises I learned from the temple priests in Bali. Definitely a more effective way to communicate privately."

"That's a relief because if Aunt Mimi heard more voices than those she already does, it could prove the tipping point."

"Naomi, I might be onto something. My dreams are talking to me. I need you to get in touch with the others and schedule a group meeting."

"That is wonderful to hear, but I may have to kill my batty aunt first."

"Put that on hold. Remember these tests the universe sends us are meant to make us smarter and stronger. More importantly, would you please send the group an email and arrange a meeting? Put

'Eureka' in the subject line. Also add, 'together we cannot be conquered.'"

"Got it, Priscilla. Meanwhile, do you have a suggestion as to what can be done about Aunt Mimi? She is delusional and taking on personas that were once part of her acting career, playing schizoid psychopaths."

"Oh dear, that does sound stressful."

"Warped would better describe it. So far, we've seen *Helga of the Third Reich*, and I'm feeling next up will be Helen Fenchurch from that series based on real life serial killers."

"*The Servant's Revenge*?"

"Yes, that's the one. What the hell can I do?"

"First of all, don't panic and let me think."

"I need a cigarette."

"Then find one and fake it. Pretend you are lighting up"

"Aunt Mimi has hidden her supply?"

"Is she on medication?"

"You name it. Bourbon, Vodka, Coca Cola and Dunhill's."

"Ah yes. The surburban cure for relief."

"Oh, and of course valium and the occasional joint."

Naomi could hear the piercing yells of her Aunt Mimi banging around on the floor above.

"Yikes! Priscilla. I think Aunt Mimi has woken up and is heading downstairs. I'm afraid Helen Fenchurch is about to confront me. I'm going to the kitchen to get a hammer."

"Naomi, first take a deep breath. I have an idea. Try this first. You remember when she played Lady Penelope Cole, the kind, old dowager in the kid's program, *Chumbley Castle*?"

"Why are you asking me this right now?"

"Do you recall the phrase she always used to calm others down?"

"Of course, I do."

"Then use it."

"What good will that do?"

"Trust me. Use it. And don't forget to send that email to the group. Talk later."

Silence. Priscilla was gone. At that moment Aunt Mimi charged into the room.

"Naomi. Where are my cigarettes?" Naomi froze.

She recognized the tone of voice. It was indeed Helen Fenchurch, the murderous housekeeper.

"Well? You do recognize a question when you hear one, don't you? And every question requires an answer. Didn't they teach you that at school? Is it necessary I should have to repeat the question for you?" snarled Aunt Mimi as Helen.

"You asked me, where are your cigarettes? Correct?" stammered Naomi.

"Correct. That is what you heard because that is what I said."

"I've no idea where they are."

"You haven't seen them."

"No."

"Have you smoked them? Because if you have smoked them, that would explain why I can't find them, and they are not where I put them last."

"No, I haven't. I mean, didn't."

"Then what have you done with them?"

"I don't recall ever seeing them."

Aunt Mimi, alias Helen Fenchurch, closed in for the kill. Drenching Naomi with a loud burp laced with vodka and rescued cigarette butts, she hissed. "You really are an ungrateful little bitch, aren't you, and not only that but a brazen liar too."

Naomi figured she could either commit murder and confess or do as Priscilla suggested. Which is what she did. Taking a deep breath. Naomi asked Helen Fenchurch.

"How about a nice cup of tea?"

The malicious glare Helen Fenchurch had fixed on Naomi melted like warm butter, replaced by the tender loving smile of her ladyship, the beloved dowager duchess Penelope Cole of Chumbley Castle. There followed a breathless moment of tension and silence before Aunt Mimi answered. "Oh. Yes, my dear, yes, that would lovely. You're such a sweet young thing. What would I do without you to help me keep the castle clean? Once the tea is served, maybe we could look at some of the old family photos together. Your darling mother Lady Parker was such a wonderful support to have around when Sir Cecil fell off the turret."

Naomi never bothered to remind Aunt Mimi that, in real life, "her darling mother" had run off with a drug lord and abandoned her when she was twelve.

"Oh, Aunt Mimi, I'm so glad to see you're feeling better. Make yourself comfortable, and I will fix you a nice cup of Earl Grey."

"How considerate you are. And so comforting."

"Would you like a chocolate biscuit with that?"

"Ooooh. I shouldn't really, but yes please."

Naomi thanked Priscilla and the Tetley tea company with a silent prayer. She had been handed the key phrase for switching Aunt Mimi's delusional roleplaying when needed. After dealing with the vicious Helga and the serial killer Helen Fenchurch, dear sweet, warm and lovable Aunt Mimi, alias, the gentle dowager was back. What did it matter if it meant drinking more tea than usual? Now Naomi could get on with what she considered her real purpose in life. She thought about the group of friends that were devoted to each other and their united cause. Cleo and Bentley for instance. Theirs was not a chance meeting. That was Kismet.

Friends Forever: Cleo and Bentley

Cleo met Bentley for the first time exiting the subway at West Fourth Street near Washington Square in Greenwich Village. The young man in his early twenties, looking somewhat like Basquiat, stood on the sidewalk addressing each and every passerby.

"Appreciate a smile. Appreciate a smile."

Most people ignored him, hurrying to where they were heading. Cleo responded to his request, and they stopped and chatted. That was long enough for Cleo to establish that Bentley had no specific agenda in life other than to make people feel better about their world. Then, almost four years later, thousands of miles from New York City, it happened again. Cleo was living in London with Evan, her boyfriend. They were not getting along well of late. She had decided to take a day of her own and explore parts of the city marked down as places to see. She was on her way to say hello to the statute of Amy Winehouse that stood among the converted horse yards, boutique shops, food stalls and bustling crowds of Camden Market. As she was exiting the nearby tube station, she heard a familiar voice.

"Appreciate a smile. Appreciate a smile."

Cleo knew that could only be Bentley.

"BibbidiBobbidi. What are you doing in Camden Town?"

Bentley showed no surprise at their encounter, as if it was destined.

"Friends invited me to housesit, and I wanted to make sure I got to visit the scene here. There is a huge mural of *The Clash*, circa "London Calling", thirty-feet high, painted on a house nearby. Must get a photo of that. What are you doing here?"

Cleo mentioned Amy Winehouse and then Bentley suggested the Hawley Arms for a pint. The Hawley was a local pub where Amy would often hang out and shoot pool after closing time. That cemented them. Cleo and Bentley became friends for life. They had revered icons in common. Extraordinary talents that had inspired so many others, in their age group. Later, seated in the patio of the Hawley Arms and enjoying the afternoon sunshine with a pint, they exchanged details of their personal backgrounds and life stories.

It turned out when Bentley realized he was gay, there had been a fleeting moment he wondered, should he have been born a woman? He briefly considered a transgender conversion but settled for a holiday in Italy instead. That solved his dilemma. He now understood he was dealing with the choice of sexual preference, not gender reversal. And he was never content to be 'gay' as in, "I'm happy". There was no apology offered. It was "I'm queer and if you disapprove, here is my middle finger stuck in the air, telling you what you can do about that." Cleo knew that Bentley would make perfect sense in the group and couldn't wait to introduce him to the others. Over a pint of Guinness, Cleo talked about the group mandate. The planet was under threat, and about to have a nervous breakdown if changes failed to be orchestrated pretty soon. She was a citizen of the world, having been born in Paris before her parents had moved to New York, when she was a baby. From there, it was Seattle, and soon after her parents decided to go their separate ways, Cleo met her boyfriend, Evan, and moved between Vancouver and New York before settling in London, living in Hackney and making extraordinary jewellery pieces from semiprecious stones, beer cans and paper clips. These she sold in local markets and on-line, providing income and the freedom to pursue her political manifesto, embracing gender rights and with groups, organizing food and medical supplies for third world countries. Together, she told Bentley they would shine a light on the world and prove, *All You Need Is Love* wasn't just an old Beatles anthem. Cleo mentioned having always had the knack of reading people's auras and what they were thinking. Sharing stories of his earlier rebel years, Bentley mentioned the time he had gone to a supermarket with a friend, after smoking a joint and etched a skull and cross-bones, with the words "Poison. Do Not Consume This Product," on boxes of kid's snacks containing high fructose corn syrup. Having left the store, at that point undetected, he went back, because he felt the artwork wasn't graphic enough, and was colouring the hollow eyes of the skull in lipstick red, when they nabbed him. He ended up doing three months of community service work. Bentley, always looking for the silver lining, saw it as a positive experience. While being assigned to wash the floors and scrub toilets in low income nursing homes for the sick and aged, he took up the guitar, wrote poetry and gave up the heavier drugs. Cleo instantly loved this "poet with a cause" and Bentley also sensed how blessed they were. Both were huge fans of classic pop. And you seldom meet someone you immediately intuit will be a friend for life, as they did. Bentley commenting; *Sweet Dreams Are Made of This*, Annie Lennox nailed it. People go looking for each other. A someone to make the journey we are all on, easier, inspiring, fun and hopefully exciting without being dangerous. There can be any number of reasons we search for that person."

"And, there are those of us who, without searching, find their other half. The pieces that should be together fall into place," Cleo added.

"Yep," Bentley replied. "Some accept that as good fortune. For others, it pops the question. Is this event preordained and synchronized?"

"Right. Like magnets drawn to each other, clicking and locking into place. And as such it would take a concerted effort to disengage."

"Like Rumi the Sufi poet said, 'Lovers don't finally meet somewhere. They're in each other all along.'"

"With no guarantee those who instantly link will find it effortless to maintain."

"It ain't always a bowl of cherries. Or without disappointment," added Bentley. "You work to make it come together.

"John Lennon." Cleo smiled.

"Accepting pieces fit but sometimes finding when the hinges get rusty..."

"...Loving care and maintenance is required."

"Either way, love is a jigsaw."

"Totally worth the risk," they chorused in unison.

Agreeing in sync, they committed to what can only be described as 'a marriage of friendship forever,' vow.

"Would you like another? It's my round."

"A pint of Guinness."

"Awesome."

The Birth of an 'Ugly Baby.'

Glancing through the back pages of the scrapbook, Bernard could vouch for his sister having always proved fearless, like an astronaut venturing into the unknown. And once she decided to break from the acceptance of academia, she was a free spirit and not about to be diverted from the urgent issues she felt needed to be addressed. Priscilla practiced pioneering where few would ever dare to tread alone. And although her expectations often found her feeling frustrated, she never gave up. She knew certain questions would remain unanswered until the day she did it herself. Death is death; that's all there is to it. Or was it? Having read many books and after countless hours in conversation with Bernard and mentors debating the subject, she was convinced there must be a way to trace a digital path, explore, breakthrough and get back safely. And Priscilla wasn't about to stand still waiting for a train to arrive to take her to the destination. She would have hopped on a plane to the "other side" at the drop of a hat, if an airline had flown there. "You can't know what you will find until you get there but failing to find out what might be waiting for you, is like going on vacation without first checking the brochure."

For Priscilla, actively listening to your own common sense before you ventured forth was mandatory. "Listening to our mind's eye will encourage us to hear the inner voice of consciousness. It will cultivate perception beyond ordinary sight. Men and women who truly listen and talk to each other make the difference."

Bernard fondly remembered the initial discussions Priscilla chaired at those early university gatherings. At first attended by only a few, the word quickly spread, and soon the small venues were overflowing. Those in attendance in rapt attention and inspired by her words.

"We are bombarded with constant noise. The noise of machines in the home and on the streets. The noise created by our daily chores. The noise of what we are told is important by the media. A never-ending babble on social networks and the airwaves every second of every day developing in us an appetite for distraction. Creating a fog in our brains. Too many talkers and not enough listeners. Why permit the dictators and bullies of this world to determine what we do and think? We need to tune into what our own intuition is telling us. Any questions?"

"What do you suggest we do to awaken this intelligence?"

"Most importantly, avoid the mystical mumbo-jumbo often associated with doing that."

"Can you elaborate"

And so, Priscilla did.

"At the beginning, I was compelled to follow each and every path that promised inspiration and enlightenment. Among them; the effort to induce a prophetic trance by inhaling the smoke from a cauldron of bubbling, mashed barley, ivy, and sacred herbs. Having a conversation with the wind. Interpreting the undines in their underwater cities, dropping LSD, reading clouds, talking to willow trees, and chewing acorns. Following that, determined to suspend time itself, I imported acacia shrub seeds from Madagascar, ground them into a flour, baked them in a cake, and ate it. This, I washed down with what I will call a Harry Potter Milkshake. An obnoxious tasting potion made from the remaining paste, muddled together with laurel, hellebore, amanita mushroom and sweetened with honey. It provided moments of the most extraordinary high but no real answers. And I must emphasise, not recommended."

Acknowledging it was a vital part of becoming a qualified explorer, Priscilla supported experimenting with caution. The curiosity that compelled new voyagers into unfamiliar territory for the betterment of human kind demanded intensive research and education. Then she mentioned an unexpected and possible avenue of reward.

"Innovation that occurs via discovery by accident. It can profoundly change the world."

Priscilla continued, while sharing this example of a personal experience, "Most of you will be surprised to find out one of my favourite pastimes is watching old movies, particularly musicals. For me, it serves as a wonderful way to unwind and relax. And I get to sing off-key without disturbing the neighbours! On this particular occasion, Frank Sinatra and Bing Crosby were trading lines in a duet from a movie called *High Society*. The next day, purely by chance, I was talking to a friend who told me *High Society* was a remake of an earlier non-musical movie named *The Philadelphia Story*. Having no idea at the time where it would lead me, I googled for details of this older film and in error, hit the link for *The Philadelphia Experiment* instead of *The Philadelphia Story*. And other than the fact, the two share the name of the same geographical location, they have nothing to do with each other. *The Philadelphia Experiment* involved the supposed disappearance of the USS Eldridge in 1944 before it mysteriously vanished, only to later reappear in New York harbour, having dematerialized, travelled through time and space and reformed at the mouth of the Hudson River. Rumours have it teleported to other dimensions, possibly involving aliens and other urban myths. Most of which were unproven, beyond belief and qualified as the most unlikely military experiment ever carried out by the U.S. Navy. Nevertheless, whether true or false, in part or whole, I was hooked on the possibilities the story presented. Provoking my interest into what might be accomplished some time, even in the near future, by the ability to move molecules through space without physical transportation and then reassemble them. Maybe, I speculated, that is how the pyramids were constructed, and let's not forget the Parthenon, Stonehenge, and similar phenomenal ancient architecture. And whether these were achieved by sheer willpower and propelled by faith towards a common goal, or if in fact, minds before ours have moved mountains without lifting a finger, why shouldn't we? The theories were endless, but most fell short of being tangible unless one speculated UFOs being involved. And then after exhausting possibilities, the obvious one path to me was self-realization and developing the latent intelligence of the third eye. I became convinced it sheltered an untapped resource for human progress."

The discussion spiralled. There were a lot of questions to be asked and answered. What was established for one and all was that Priscilla was a born leader. A brilliant scientific physicist and anthropologist, having aced every exam and challenge any university could throw at her, she was encouraging the commitment of those attending to venture outside their present mode of docile acceptance. Find new solutions for the distribution of wealth and resources. Restructure how we deal with the problems that face the planet and the people who live on it.

"And it is only fair to say stepping onto uncharted territory can mean finding yourself leaving the only footprint in the sand. It is important to form alliances with like-minded people. Selectively build small units based on common objectives and trust. Then let the world know we are here. Be brave and outspoken about it. Nobody out there is waiting to pin a medal on you. Or hand you a diploma."

A voice from among the audience spoke up, "What should we call ourselves?"

"One suggestion is to think of yourselves as ugly babies. Not to be coddled and made a fuss over. Or distracted by new toys and pacifiers. Quite the contrary. Rather, know you will be pushed aside, ridiculed and ignored. It is not our quest to seek approval from those who got us into this mess. They are lost. It is our job to encourage those who might listen and join us to make changes. So, at first accept and prepare to be treated as an ugly baby. No one is going to want to attend to you crying. It will take strong affirmative action before we are recognized as having grown into responsible administrators. Fulfilling the beautiful intuitive people we are to become. I highly recommend you commit to supporting each other and saving the planet."

Many, Many, Happy Returns! Meet Janet

At the back of the room that day, Janet Green sat paying close attention to the younger woman leading the discussion. She had heard Priscilla was an emerging force and strong advocate for necessary change.

After the lecture, Janet suggested they go for a coffee. It was a meeting meant to be. As if one shoe had been searching for the other, making sure they walked side by side in the same direction. Following a number of meetings and conversations over coffee, food and wine, they formed a bond and outlined a plan.

Janet would fill the role of Project Mother and be consulted before decisions involving strategy were decided. She was expert in effective social networking, weeding out fake news, manipulative broadcast politics and popular gossip. Getting dependable facts from fiction. And generating a warm curiosity. What else could one say to describe Janet. Hmmm? She would likely have been a Woodstock child. Flowers in her hair. With several unique anomalies. Serving as an outstanding example of this, Janet claimed more birthdays every year than any other person Priscilla had ever met. By mid-October, after meeting at the university forums in February, Janet had announced at least four birthdays. And it surely wasn't because Janet enjoyed being considered the wise elder. However, if you were to say, "Hey Janet, *The Tangled Conkers* (her favourite group), are playing at the Palladium, September 8th. Do you wanna go?" Chances are Janet would respond, "Oh. Yes. Perfect. That's my birthday!" It was like trying to determine what number ball was going to fall from an air bingo machine, until one of them dropped by chance. The fact being, if the birthdays Janet regularly announced were true, it would put her age between one hundred and fifty-four and two hundred and forty-seven.

One explanation, as Priscilla had duly noted, was when Janet acquired any significant piece of information for the very first time, she claimed it as a birth date for herself of the occasion. For instance, one day when she and Janet were shopping for plants, Mr. Willard, who runs the local gardening store, was asked by a customer as to the best month and season to sow a row of winter cabbages and how far apart they should be. He replied, "You can plant drum head red cabbage from mid-summer up until early fall. I recommend sowing them twelve inches apart and having them firmly planted by September fifteenth." Janet, on hearing this, piped up, "Oh, that's my birthday," and everyone in the little shop stopped and smiled at her. Two shoppers as though it meant something to them, actually applauded! Yet Janet knew, Priscilla knew, that it wasn't her real birthday. So, what was her reason for saying it? Priscilla pondered that it might have something to do with a theory of constant rebirth. And that possibly having more birthdays than Methuselah contributed to a perpetual youthful demeanour and appearance. Similar to Andy Warhol who began wearing a white wig from age twenty-five onwards, so that his appearance belied his years. Most certainly, Janet did not want to look as old as the birthdays she claimed to have. Nevertheless, she persisted. Priscilla explained to the rest of the group in confidence, "If you happen to be around when Janet announces that it's her birthday, just say; "Many, Many, Happy Returns, Janet."

That could be said about Janet. Nobody would ever want to miss one of her birthdays and hurt her feelings.

* * *

The email Priscilla had asked Naomi to send, addressed only to their small group, would change their lives forever. Looking around the room on the day the meeting took place, with close friends gathered, Bernard smiled with pride. Priscilla was once again weaving her persuasive research into a rallying call. Everybody who had been sent the invitation attended. Expectations were high. Dedicated people seeking to develop new methods for dealing with derelict models. That quest had drawn them together in the first place. Naomi, her dedicated champion; Cleo;

who worked for the outreach of the International Women and Children's Relief Organizations; Bentley, an intuitive poet and newest recruit, advocating gender equality and LGBTQ rights; Janet, the eldest, a social media IT networking expert and; Bernard, her older sibling and guardian watchdog. All loyal and trusted friends. Their united endeavour was to implement solutions addressing the issues threatening the planet. Which meant, confronting the lack of education, the lack of accountability of rogue governments and blatant corruption. Set in motion by a comparatively few elected individuals and creating poverty, hunger, oppression, racism and war for the many. Priscilla opened the meeting.

"For us 'ugly babies' to make a real change in this crazy world, we must be prepared and equipped for the exploration, breaking through, strategically retreating if necessary, but…never capitulating."

The progress made to date Priscilla was willing to share, but only if based on the contribution of each member justified her doing that. Which meant individually developing the skills and endurance required for the journey. Priscilla told us why she committed to training her inner eye. She handed each of us a U.S. one-dollar bill and posited that developing the higher intelligence of the mind's eye was part of an earlier vision, designed by the group known as the Founding Fathers of the American Revolution.

"Consider the symbols and the printed words. Besides the eagle grasping the arrows in its talons, there is a truncated pyramid with the omniscient eye and the motto 'Novus Ordo Seclorum' heralding, 'A New Order of The Ages.'". The subtext of the dollar bill says it loud and clear. "Let us move forward together to build a brave new world."

However, the term "Founding Fathers", also struck many as inherently sexist, verbally excluding women from a prominent role in the formation. Influential women, such as Abigail Adams, Dolley Madison, and Mercy Otis Warren, all made significant contributions that merit attention. And that label undermines their role. Which may account for the "Novus Ordo Seclorum" turning out to be something of a current train wreck the planet was trying to avoid. Priscilla proposed it was time to revise that order. Among the key notes Priscilla conveyed were the importance of holding up the mirror to ourselves and realizing the planet was in real trouble. Emphasizing we should get up each day and do what we are able to do, in whatever way we could. Promote clean renewable energy, as opposed to fossil fuels, pesticides, and chemicals. Protect all people and communities and support their indigenous land rights activities. Stop the killing of environmental defenders. Prosecute their attackers. Cherish the land, protect natural resources and wildlife. In short, wake up and take action.

"We should think of ourselves as the points of a star moving forward together, spearheading a revolutionary awareness that cannot be ignored. Forging a safer path for humankind. A new era for living amazing lives that matter. Nature is showing increasing signs of stress because of our self-absorbed, grasping, greedy and know-it-all behaviour. Mother Earth is not a video game where the tough guys, after mistreating women, children and each other, engage in a final shootout to establish the top dog. It's been calculated we are using two percent or less of our brain potential. Whatever is not being used must surely be capable of telling us something."

Using a visual presentation, charts and research, Priscilla provided a compelling picture. Ancient cultures who knew more about the potential of the brain than many of us. For instance, Polynesian navigators mapped out most of the terrain of the Pacific Ocean in canoes. Certainly, they used some crude wooden instruments, but mostly they relied on an oral tradition, often in the form of song with close observation of the sea, the flight of various species of birds, the winds, the waves and what the sky and clouds were telling them. Techniques and traditions that were passed from master to apprentice. And, word has it, they might have made touchdown in America before Columbus did. When you consider that in those times people believed the world was flat, can you imagine how scary a voyage on thousands of miles of uncharted waters would be. Knowing you might possibly fall off the ends of the earth? That is truly taking a trip into the unknown. And they did this paddling in canoes. And that was the point she made for the group.

If we don't allow ourselves to venture into the unknown, knowing we might possibly fail, we will never create new solutions to the ongoing problems we have created. We should accept possible setbacks as part of our awakening. Because without it, we are just going to spin around the same issues, repeat the same mistakes and find out too late that the knowledge we keep accumulating and applying with one blind eye, is destroying us and this extraordinary planet we live on.

Priscilla suggested a good question to ask oneself. "What makes us so proud to demonstrate and celebrate violence, often gender-based violence? Is that any way to treat your mother who gave birth to you?

Ahhh. I think not. The world is limitless. Just listen and observe. The inner ear and the inner eye are yours to explore. Activate your intuition and start seeing from the inside out. Don't allow yourself to be led around by a ring someone has stuck in your nose. They're feeding you whatever advances their personal financial or political agenda with information cooked up by them explicitly for that purpose. Enriching themselves at your expense. Generating twisted or false facts, building distorted algorithms based on how you respond to their manipulation. Their plans are designed to dislodge you from your own path. To confuse and then recruit you to join them. That ring they stuck in your nose is not going to lead you to a better world. Practice mindfulness. Not mindlessness. The potential to make a truly big difference is within each and every one of us. In fact, staring us in the face when we look in the mirror."

Priscilla outlined a program to guide us. Suggesting, if it was accepted, we would disband for six months and meet again at the summer equinox, providing we felt we were ready to move on to the next stage. Her program contained simple guidelines and outlined the following exercises:

Train the mind's eye to acquire active listening and focused intelligence. This is the foundation for pre- telekinesis ability.

Work on the exercises given to rearrange molecules and move small objects in space.

Develop an intuitive ability to understand what someone is thinking. As opposed to what they may say.

Priscilla described her personal experience. "The first steps that worked for me should work for you also. But you must verify each of them for yourself. My first attempts after contacting Naomi in an early successful mind-wave connection, were to move objects at a distance by mental power or other non-physical means. Sitting at the kitchen table, I began manipulating the paper cup in front of me and then moved on to heavier, larger objects. Applying the triangular energy of my third eye, I managed to transmute the object I focused on. Initially, appearing as a signal similar to a television screen scrambling a transmission. Followed by the gradual breaking down and disappearance of the object itself."

Realizing she was able to alter and shape the atoms and molecules of energy and matter, Priscilla kept working in concentrated intervals, taking rests in between. She worked on a wooden chair. At first it was one leg or a portion she transposed. With practice she was successful in making the whole chair disappear, leaving everything else in the room intact. It didn't change anything else in her immediate environment, and after she relaxed, the chair was back intact where it belonged. Priscilla had managed to harness the ability to carry out telekinesis. Still the question remained; during the moment of rearranging the particles of the physical object where had the object gone? And then, how could objective teleportation be activated? If she could resolve that, then the possibilities were infinite. She had considered contacting the others at that point, but after second thoughts decided to press on until questions could be answered with facts. Now, having called this meeting before discussing future possibilities, Priscilla asked for a commitment 'to go together where no one had ventured before.' It wasn't going to be easy.

But as Bentley pointed out, "Is there a better way to spend time in your life than with people you love, who care about each other, drinking an occasional Kombucha martini while munching on lots of healthy hors d'oeuvres?"

Priscilla put it to a show of hands for approval. The arms shot up in unison. A unanimous agreement was reached. We signed on as Ugly Babies to set sail into unchartered waters together. We had no idea that Priscilla would acquire a book picked up by Cleo in London, embarking on two experiments that would change not only the immediate group's lives forever. The potential accomplishment for human mind development would never be the same.

The Southbank Book Fair

Living in London, Cleo had recently broken up with her boyfriend Evan and settled into a single life, keeping her jewellery business in order while maintaining contact with close friends. Life was no longer about making money, and it wasn't about Evan and trying to understand why he was such a loser. She understood that every girl dreams of being a woman, and a woman has to keep that girl inside alive. But a partner exercising his control over her was not romantic. A lover with no strings could make her world go around for the time being. Cleo had been working on her mind's eye exercises for some time. She now felt she was capable of seeing beneath and beyond the surface of the material world. That's when Priscilla called asking her to locate a unique book.

"What makes it unique?"

"It will only reveal its contents to the chosen individual"

Cleo was understandably sceptical about this statement.

"Priscilla, this book has information only you alone can access?"

"The formulae it contains will not be understood by anybody else."

"Who told you that?"

"The voice inside my head told me."

"You heard yourself telling yourself... what exactly?"

"To contact Cleo and have her pick up a book that is waiting for me at the book fair being held outside The National Theatre on the Southbank."

"So, I've been elected to pick it up, and it has your name on it?"

"Intuitively, I understand I'm the only person it will allow to decipher ALL of the content. So, in that sense, it has my name on it."

"And it will make itself known to me on your behalf?"

"Correct."

"And the name of this tome?"

"*The Teleporter's Handbook.*"

All of which, at the very best, sounded sketchy. However, Cleo trusted Priscilla knew what she was talking about. And she reasoned, from Queen Boadicea, up to and including the present day, much of what had made Britain "Great" was courtesy of the women warriors and queens that challenged and often ruled the history of those islands.

* * *

It was a perfect day for the stroll along the pathway of the South Bank beside the River Thames. When you are in London, it is one of the most magical places to spend a day. From any one of the many bridges, you can see the River Thames winding through various parts of the city and sights. Cleo decided to start at London Bridge and visit Southwark Cathedral. Five hundred years ago this was where the heads of tyrants, traitors, political prisoners and some plain unfortunates, would be displayed after being chopped off in the nearby Tower of London. Thankfully, no sign of them today. She walked down the stone steps and joined the crowd in the bustling Borough Market. Priscilla had assigned her a task, and whatever the outcome, she was going to enjoy the experience.

On her way to the National Theatre Book Fair, she would pass the remnants of Winchester Palace, a twelfth century abbey, that had once served as a townhouse for the Bishops of Winchester. Where in time past, sheltered by the darkened archways of the river, a flock of women, known as the "Winchester Geese", would be found plying their sex trade in the nearby rowdy ale taverns and doss houses. Approved by the clergy, they provided a lucrative tax income for the church upkeep and maintenance. They were also, the acknowledged source of 'goose bumps'; you wouldn't want to catch…

Keep moving along the cobble streets, past the Clink Prison Museum and several cozy old pubs. Past the Globe Theatre, a reconstruction accomplished in wonderful detail by American actor-director Sam Wanamaker, where audiences today enjoy classical plays in progress. Cleo could see the Millennium Bridge ahead and made note to visit The Tate Modern, which had recently added a new extension to the original makeover of a disused power station. People were strolling across the bridge from St Paul's Cathedral or alternatively leaving The Tate to walk across the bridge to the city business area. The London Eye, Big Ben, and Westminster Abbey lay up ahead and she made note to visit those on another day.

Cleo was now approaching the stacked tables outside the National Theatre Bar where people sat and drank a glass of whatever they chose, to pass a glorious sunny afternoon. She saw clusters of people searching tables, and obviously this was the book sale event. She stood idling at the rows of trestle tables full of books without knowing how to identify what she was looking for. Taking place almost every weekend, this Saturday was a special fund raiser for the SPCTA. The Brits have always had fondness for their pets and gardens, preferring them to certain people and often each other. Cleo mused on this thought as she began to look at thousands of books being riffled through, most them discarded without paying close attention, in favour of a new search.

After her walk, Cleo thought it would good to relax, get herself a drink and sit at one of the patio tables. That would allow her to observe what was going on with the rummaging and selling of books close by. With a view of the city across the Thames, she sat drinking a glass of prosecco on tap and watched the prospective book buyers making impulse decisions about books and authors. To buy or not? Reading them cover to cover would be for another day. Cleo observed until she sensed it was time to employ her third eye to locate what she was looking for. A second glass of wine crossed her mind and as much as she would have liked that, maybe later. Without prior notice, a book in the pile on one of the nearest tables caught her attention. She didn't read the title; she just heard a voice in her head say.

"Pick me up." Cleo picked the book up, opened the cover and heard the voice again.

"Now, put me down. It's not me. What you're looking for is over there."

She put the book down and then picked it back up, deciding she was the reader and this was only a book. The book voice spoke again. This time with clarity and emphasis, "I said, put me back. It's not me. Look over there!"

Cleo scanned two dozen long, extended trestle tables crammed with books, and people briefly checking out covers and may be a page or two and then moving on to the next. It was a paper jungle of titles with some engaging and bizarre topics. How was she going to recognize what Priscilla had sent her to find? Then she heard the voice again.

"Go to the seventh table, third book on the right. You will see a light flickering from within." Cleo focused on that table, and sure enough, one book nestled among many others began to glow on and off. She quickly headed toward it before it was claimed by someone else. She picked the book up. There was no title. She opened it. The pages were blank. Then the book voice spoke, "Find a quiet spot. Get me out of here."

Cleo could sense shapes and symbols almost like electronic figures dancing in the background of vacant pages. She attempted to decipher what they said, but they began to scramble whatever they might have meant to her. The words vanished, and the pages were empty. The book voice spoke again. This time louder and emphatic, "I said, get me outta here!"

This had to be the book Priscilla wanted her to locate. Cleo found a quiet spot on a bench a little away from the busy tables. She began to wonder whether her mind's eye was creating an hallucination. At that moment, letters spelling out the title on the front cover appeared.

The Teleporter's Handbook

Ping!

The book opened. Words appeared on the preface page stating;

Please note you have five minutes to read the content outline of this book before it vanishes and will no longer reveal the words within unless the reader has been approved. The turn of pages will be announced by a small bell and then proceed to the next page. This is a truth that cannot be tamed.

Cleo questioned whether this was really happening.

Ping! The pleasant bell sounded again. The book turned itself to the next page and the following words dropped into place:

The Teleporter's Handbook

Chapter One: The Awakening:

One day when God was chomping on a cob of corn, some of the kernels fell into endless space and that is how the planets were formed. The End.

Cleo was thinking that must be the shortest story she had ever read when…Ping! The light lit up and the page of the book turned.

Chapter Two: Potions and Lotions

You can try any concoction you want to. Hopefully it doesn't upset your tummy, but reading the next chapter should eliminate the need to ingest horrendous drinks or rub frog's puke on your skin or similar.

Ping! The light lit up and the page turned by itself again.

Chapter Three: Developing the Third Eye or Mind's Eye

*IMPORTANT! This is an unseen eye that provides perception beyond ordinary sight. Known to be the gateway leading to the inner realms and spaces of higher consciousness. It comes with a responsibility and even initially can enable a state of enlightenment, reading auras and clairvoyance. And is capable of observing objects as small as quarks.**

**A quark is an elementary particle and a fundamental constituent of matter. Quarks combine to form composite particles called hadrons, the most stable of which are protons and neutrons, the components of atomic nuclei.*

Ping! The light lit up and the page, once again, turned over.

Chapter Four: Telekinesis

Psychokinesis is an alternative term also often used for this. The user can acquire capabilities to influence, manipulate, move objects and matter with their mind at various levels. Telekinesis is one of the powers that are based on controlling and manipulating. It may evolve to the point that a Telekinetic person can control anything at a subatomic, particle and universal level.

Ping! And Yes. Cleo marvelled as the light lit up and the page once again, flipped itself over. She could hardly believe the process she was experiencing. At that moment, a smartly dressed lady walked by with a small scotch terrier, on a leash, clad in a tartan weather jacket. The dog stopped and began sniffing around. Cleo was about close the book and put it back when the book voice spoke again.

"Do not close or put me down." This time the woman heard it and the dog growled.

"Robertson," the woman said, addressing the small terrier. "Be nice."

The woman took a step back and gave Cleo a challenging stare. Cleo ignored her and carried on as though she hadn't heard a thing. The woman and the dog left the scene. Both had their noses in the air. The book's voice resumed listing its outline.

Ping!

Chapter Five: Teleportation

Dematerializing, followed by the transfer of matter or energy from one location to another without traversing the physical space between them. By means of quantum entanglement when two particles having the same existence are created at the same time and place, if one of the photons is changed, then the other photon in the other location changes too.

Close by, two noisy teenagers and their parents were arguing about what exhibit they should visit next.

"The London Eye. The Eye," the elder one yelled.

"No, Buckingham Palace," said the other. "You promised."

Priscilla refocused her mind's eye attempting to capture a photograph of the information of each page as it turned.

Ping!

Chapter Six: Invisibility

This is made possible by creating a cloak. Bending electromagnetic radiation, such as light, around an object giving the appearance that it isn't there at all. Think of it as a river running around a stone and continuing to flow without having registered the change. The formula for the required meta materials is as follows.

A series of jumbled formulae appeared and began fading as a shadow loomed over the book. A rude voice demanded Cleo's attention..

"Are you going to buy that book or not? Having you paw the pages will not make it more attractive to potential buyers. And if it is taking this long for you to browse through, it must be worth buying, wouldn't you say?"

"Not really, there is nothing in it."

"What do you mean?"

"Take a look for yourself. The pages are all blank."

The grouchy attendant grabbed the book from Cleo's hand and flipped through the empty pages. "Ridiculous. What made it so interesting in the first place?"

"It spoke to me."

"Oh, you're one of those, 'it spoke to me,' people."

"Yes, it spoke to me."

"And what did it say?"

"That's between me and the book. What is it saying to you?"

"It's saying you are possibly a book thief and should either buy it or move along because we can't afford to have any more books go missing."

"Well, if you changed the way you talk to potential customers then books that go missing wouldn't be your second biggest problem."

"You're not a customer yet. You haven't bought anything."

"Okay, how much is this worth?"

"Five pounds."

"Five pounds with nothing on the pages?"

"If it talks to you, then five pounds is a cheap price to pay, and you can imagine whatever you want on the pages. They appear untouched, except for your fingerprints."

"You know, you're right. That's a cheap price to pay for such an unusual book. I'm going to give you twenty for it. You can keep the change, on one condition. Try being pleasant with other customers you talk to. You will sell more books" Cleo handed him a twenty pound note. "Have a nice day."

Cleo strode off with the book, walking along the South Bank clutching a priceless treasure. "Mission accomplished," she whispered to herself.

"Well done," the book said.

"Thank you," said Cleo. "What else can you tell me?"

"There's a lot of work before we get you rearranging molecules and moving mountains."

"Anything after that?"

"Invisibility and time travel."

"I can't wait"

"Our allotted time is running out."

"Can I make a copy of you?"

"Access is now prohibited."

PING!

The pages of the book showed only fading letters of the alphabet. Then nothing.

The Talbot Residence. Windstone. The Second Experiment

Having acquired the book from Cleo, after carefully following the diagrams, codes and equations the book revealed, Priscilla proceeded step by step, progressing from the basic levels of levitation, the pull and push of objects around an orbital field, and then began working on the formula procedures for invisibility and teleportation. If succesful, she could only imagine the barrage of questions that would likely follow. An obvious one would be;

"What if it fell into the wrong hands and was used destructively?"

She understood why the book protected itself from those readers not ready to assimilate the content.

Many of the questions would only be answered at a future time. For Priscilla what needed to be resolved was figuring out how one teleports rearranged molecules. Once proven, the potential was virtually limitless. It was that day after successfully solving the invisibility formula. She was feeling well rested, peaceful. And once again, standing on the upstairs balcony of the old summer house, Priscilla was looking at the cherry tree below and the field beyond, surrounding the family property. She had spent so many summers here growing up. The cherry tree stood where it had always stood for the past thirty years. Leaving everything around it recognisable and intact, Priscilla was attempting to deconstruct and teleport the molecules of the tree, and reform it elsewhere, yet close by. A 'before and after' snapshot of the scene would look like this: Before; would show you the cherry tree with the fence and fields behind it. After; would show the same fence and fields, except in place of the cherry tree, an empty space where it had once stood. Focusing her third eye she transmitted the small triangular star of five energy points to the designated object. The branches and trunk of the old cherry tree wavered, momentarily scrambled, rearranged its structure and then was gone. Abracadabra and Holy Moly! The cherry tree was no longer there.

Priscilla held the moment in focus and shifted her attention to where she had intended to teleport the tree. Instinctively she ran to the front of the house and there it was. Mission accomplished! She had deconstructed and transported the tree intact from one place to another. Priscilla stayed in the moment, took a snapshot with her mind, reversed the applied equation, then disconnecting from her third eye, blinked and brought the tree back to where it had always stood. Mission completed. How to explain this to her friends? She was overjoyed and wanted to share these moments. More importantly, would they be willing to keep working and developing together as a group? There were still stages of progress she needed to prove, before going into the world at large to put what she had researched and experienced to the test. Priscilla decided to head into the village the next day and see if she could dematerialize, teleport, and reform a car or vehicle to a different and designated location.

* * *

Meanwhile, not having heard from his sister in some time, Bernard was growing concerned

"What the hell is she up to now?" he wondered.

Several weeks had passed since anyone had heard a word from her. Knowing Priscilla could look after herself, at first Bernard was not too worried. Then further articles, slanted to disparage his sister's opinions and ambitions, began rapidly surfacing in both the social and broadcast media. Comments suggested she might be better off living elsewhere and benefit from consulting a psychiatrist before she did further damage. Bernard left an urgent message on the private cell phone only Priscilla and he shared. He didn't wait long before she replied.

"Hey, little sister. Checking in, wondering what you were up to."

"Too much to tell you in one call, dear brother. Brevity and complete discretion are the key factors for the time being. Don't worry, I will elude capture before the hyenas arrive at my door. I'm working on a way to camouflage detection and hide in plain sight."

Bernard sensed whatever Priscilla had accomplished, spelled trouble ahead.

"Priscilla, be careful chopping down monsters. They don't fall easy. And can cause an awful lot of problems and noise before they cave."

"Got that. Bernard, I need you to get some information for me. Contact Janet in L.A. Avoid the direct use of my name during the conversation. Ask her what convincing identity manipulation might involve if it should become necessary in the near future. Some real progress being made but I'm still working with results that need confirmation and protection. Proof my research can be verified for the benefit of a future generation. So, before the corporate dinosaurs bag me for questioning, I need to stay low. Recently, colleagues from my university days were interviewed about my activities and whereabouts, using methods that were impolite and outside of the accepted protocol. Which means, I am targeted and if they find me, will be detained. So, we might be wise to create a batch of red herrings. Actually, make those purple! Buy some time. So, I can look at all possible options and feel confident we are ready to counter-attack. Meanwhile, and this is very important, tell Janet to kiss the babies for me and let the 'nursery' know, for the time being, we are going to C.R."

C.R. Close ranks. Once again, Priscilla was dancing in and around a situation that was heading along a path only she had the map for. The problem for everyone involved, including herself being, 'the map was not the territory.' The territory may have been sketched by research for group benefit but had yet to be proven and confirmed. However, the message was clearly understood. They were being tracked and under surveillance. There was no other option but to 'close ranks'. On the pretext of calling about advice for a business client. Bernard called Janet.

"Hello Janet."

"Hello Bernard. What's up?"

"Wondering if you can help me with some advice."

"Concerning?"

"A friend of mine considering having work done without identity attached. Is there a name for that kind of work?"

"Botox or Post Botox. That kind of work...?"

"A makeover - possible?"

"All is possible. What did you advise?"

"Why are they even bothering? They have a perfectly lovely manner and look great."

"So they need a new passport?"

"I'm not sure if they are that desperate."

"You wouldn't say that if you lived in Los Angeles."

"Why is that?"

"Everyone here is appearance and identity obsessed."

"I do understand it must be a confidence booster to look good. Question: is there a way of camouflaging without reconstructing your appearance? Temporary masking?"

"Wear wigs and move to a remote location."

"That's a thought"

"Well, whatever it is they're thinking of doing, tell them to consider it carefully before they go ahead. I've seen some powerful execs and celebrities who went from beauty to botched and paid enormous amounts for the privilege."

"My friend doesn't have wads of money to spend. What happens if the surgeon messes it up?"

"That would be classified as a minor botch."

"A minor botch. What is 'a minor botch' in that line of work?"

"A minor botch is like one eye looking slightly larger or elevated. Or a twisted lip. I've seen some botch jobs that were truly interesting.".

"Ugh. The end result being…?."

"Sometimes, it improves that person's social life."

"Really. How so?"

"People in a similar circle will invite you to their dinner parties to observe and discuss the botch and then offer opinions and suggestions as to what you might do about it. And the food can be great. Avocado papaya salads and smart cocktails etc Meeting new friends."

"Sounds like an art gallery reception."

"It's Los Angeles."

"And what kind of opinions and suggestions would they likely offer?"

"Where you should have gone, instead of where you did. Who might have done a better job. Who you might consult to fix the botch job. And what that will likely cost."

"Wouldn't that advice be more helpful if one knew that beforehand?"

"I suppose so, but people here are very guarded about their cosmetic practitioners. Everyone is sworn to secrecy."

"Unless you're the victim, it seems."

"Give me specific details. I will get back to you with the best options possible."

"Hmm. Maybe it would be better sending my friend to a holistic internist instead."

"That's a thought. You can always find a fresh duck quacking in a new age pond."

"Janet, I think you should move out of that city. It sounds like a bizarre human zoo where you wander around among some dangerous animals turned loose and on the prowl. Snacking on the less fortunate."

"I don't hang out with these types often as you well know Bernard. They have no idea what I get up to with my real friends."

"Hey, Janet, thanks. You've been very helpful. Before we sign off, have you heard from Priscilla recently?"

"She did contact me briefly a while back to get some data information, but it was a short conversation."

"Typical Priscilla. Let her know her brother is trying to reach her if you reach her before I do. Oh, and let the babies know we're okay."

"Will do that. I will give Naomi a call."

"Okay, Janet. Until then. We're C.R. Take care. Talk soon."

"Got it. Bye, Bernard."

CLICK. Janet closed that call and pondered… closing ranks. What was Priscilla up to? She had noted a surge in social media exchanges that were building a negative profile around Priscilla's activities. Prying and provoking and colouring the facts. Obviously, her strategy to unglue the power leeches, was working. She was getting under their skin. Bernard conveying the message to "close ranks" meant there were new developments. Fast dial Naomi. Maybe she knew something but even if she didn't, anyone tracking the call would end up more confused than enlightened.

BRRIING. BRIINNGG!

"Hullo."

"Hi Naomi. We're C.R. What's cooking in the kitchen."

"Janet! Solo dinner takeout chow mien with prawns. Care to join me?"

"I'm sooo hungry, but it's too far. Let's make a date for the next opportunity."

"Okay, Naomi, and before your noodles go cold and gummy, have you heard from Priscilla?'

"Ahhhm. One very elusive abrupt exchange."

"And…?"

"She was absolutely convinced our text and email exchanges are tapped. Insists we are being tracked for our activities and refuses to do Facebook etc. So, is reluctant to have a decent chat about anything."

"And…"

"She wanted to find out what I knew about canoeing."

"Canoeing!?"

"It would seem she has a yen to hang out in the wilderness with the loons."

"Maybe, she needs a vacation."

"She did ask how my yoga and meditation sessions were progressing."

"What did you tell her?"

"I told her I had successfully got rid of a problem by drinking more tea with Aunt Mimi. And that her advice, in general, was very helpful in stopping me taking up smoking again. Plus, I'd had some success making an old lover disappear, and so it was definitely improving my ability to clean out some of the B.S. Then we chatted for a bit about Silicon Valley avenues of research and then she ended the call. Rather abruptly as she is prone to do."

"Typical Priscilla, she hates telephones and social media. Thinks they are all controlled by rings of spies."

"Oh dear. Priscilla and her wacky theories."

"She really believes we can reach the moon without a space ship."

"What!"

"She was also alluding to developing the process of living forever."

"Wang dang doodle!"

"Oh, and she chats with her intuition daily. And it tells her what to do. She mentioned sending Cleo on a book search in London. Like I said, the subject of our phone chat did some hip-hop and slide, before ending abruptly."

"Hmm. Look Janet. If she contacts you again, tell her I must speak to her. It's urgent. My Aunt Mimi is bat crackers, and I am only the person that she will allow in the house to look after her. Priscilla helped me out recently and now I'm looking for a follow up consultation."

"Bernard called wanting to talk to Priscilla also. Asking questions about makeover magicians in L.A."

"What did you tell him?"

"One on every corner."

"Okay. Now Janet, don't YOU go messing with that sweet face of yours."

"You can request your favourite music tracks while they are going about their job."

"Might I suggest, 'The First Cut is The Deepest'?"

"You've still got that edgy sense of humour, Naomi."

"Thank you."

"And, by the way, my face is not going anywhere near a knife."

"Smart girl. Has Priscilla mentioned a next meeting?"

"Not to me."

"Listen, my noodles are congealing. Gotta go. Give my love to the Babies."

"Okay, Naomi. Best Wishes and C.R."

"Got it. Okay, Janet, I will pass that on. Luv ya. And...take care."

"Will do. Bye."

Click. Naomi thought anybody listening into that call would certainly require a translator. But the very clear message from Priscilla was to close ranks. Hmm. Naomi sat back and thought about her friends. Recalling the last group meeting she could hear Priscilla's voice in her head.

"What have the leaders of our broken capitalism given us? Disastrous economics. Corrupt politics. Empty promises. Sabotaged support for stranded refugees and contaminated food supplies. Plus, we have inherited a crumbling ecosystem."

* * *

On that occasion, Naomi recalled the classic Sam Cooke track, *A Change is Gonna Come*, reverberating off the walls and ceiling to the cheers and applause echoing in the room. Naomi could sense there was no turning back. Finally, the strategies of power mad people running the planet were coming to an end. They had been able to create a false sense of strong government and prosperity, for the rest of us. So, while we were getting hustled, they were getting rich.

"Their time was up."

Priscilla was seeking a way to recover, repair and redirect their exploitation. Armed with new weapons, preparing for the battle ahead. Confounding the enemy was now mandatory. The "babies" had learned to play smart. But Priscilla would need a deck of aces to win the game now in progress.

Teleporting: Priscilla Helps a Friend

Priscilla crossed the road in the cozy village of Windstone. This is a place that looks perfect for filming those weekly murder mysteries you see on television. And like those stories, only in real life, everybody knows what everybody might be doing with somebody or each other. Priscilla was on her way to visit an old trusted friend. Hopefully he was going to allow her to teleport his food truck to another location. She had no doubt, if that was accomplished, it would be the talk in the pubs for months. There it was; she spotted the familiar truck. Not in the usual location and also sporting a flat tire. She remembered as a kid buying hot dogs from the Paul's Dogs on Wheels. Paul had been like a second older brother to her growing up. After Priscilla moved away, stories filtered down about his affair with Carol the wife of the local pub owner, Albert, who was a nasty piece of work. And of course, the local gossipmongers had a field day. She wondered if Paul still operated the same business out of the vehicle. Healthy Veggie Hot Dogs, Burgers and Fries. And ice cream floats. The old vehicle was certainly looking worse for wear, and Priscilla wanted to make sure Paul was still in business.

"Knock. Knock. Anyone home?" Priscilla was standing at the trailer door when Paul came around from the back of the trailer on crutches. A big smile on his face.

"I know that voice. I know that voice."

"Paul, it's me, Priscilla."

"Ah yes, veggie hot dog, extra cheese, and yam fries. All grown up."

"What happened here?" Priscilla said, pointing to his crutches.

"Ah, Carol's ex, Albert, had some people move into town." Paul was indicating a shop front establishment across the road. The Burger Bonanza was a business Priscilla was unfamiliar with.

"And…?"

"And one day I had an unfortunate accident."

No further explanation required. Priscilla knew why she was there.

"What needs to be done?

"Once I get rid of the crutches, Carol and I can knock him and his goon squad off their perch."

"Maybe I can help."

The Talbot Residence. One Year Later.

The relaxed sound of laughter and easy conversation. A garden party in progress. Food catered and prepared by Paul and Carol being eagerly sampled and consumed. Everyone in the group was in attendance. However, no one could be seen. It was in fact, an invisible garden party, rightfully claiming a place among the first of its kind. Cloaking unseen voices heard overlapping.

"…Oh, what a beautiful day this is.

…An invisible picnic, brilliant idea.

…Amazing spread

…What are those?

…Goat cheese appetizers and black olives.

…Delicious sandwiches. Those little curls of salmon.

…I think it's tuna.

…Yes, it's tuna.

…Must have another one or three.

…Pass me one of those salads.

…Chickpea carrot or…"

A game of badminton was in progress. The announcement of each and every point won or lost being cheered by those watching. The shuttlecock sailed high over the net between players. The racquets, dipping high and low, retrieving the feathered birdie before it touched the lawn or was left to fall out of bounds. This activity was occasionally interrupted by Brambles the cat who stalked, then chased to intercept the floating missile until he declined to participate any further, preferring to stretch and scratch his ear in the shade. From an observer's point of view, as if mirroring the badminton match, trays were floating in and out of the house and across the lawn to a large table. Chairs shifted here and there by unseen hands. Likewise, forks and spoons dipped and scooped food on plates that hovered above the tablecloth before settling into place. It was a year and a day after the meeting that established the UBO (Ugly Babies Organization). This gathering was to celebrate an international project to be carried out by its members. Bentley and Cleo were being dispatched to Somalia to help ensure the delivery and distribution of support and supplies that were not reaching those in need. Recruitment programs had been underway and new members were being appointed after passing the training program and certification. The initial trial project to curtail trophy hunters killing elephants had been successful. The local guides had refused to cooperate with the carnage after witnessing apparitions and strange behaviours, creating rumours that spread like wildfire. The majestic creatures were left in peace to roam their natural habitat, and a victory was chalked up for the UBO. But there were ever increasing problems on a much larger scale with no solution at hand. The real threat for future food production was lack of water. Supplying water for the increasing quantities of grain the world consumes. The problems of oil supply, often generating headline news masked a greater threat. There are substitutes for oil, but not for water. We can produce food without oil but not without water. Tapping underground water resources may have temporarily helped expand world food production but as demand for grain continued climbing, so also did the amount of water pumped. Leaving us on a collision course with disaster, due to over pumping, as use outstrips recharge. A sombre thought to consider on a sunny day. Only to be further underlined by Priscilla's voice interrupting the celebration.

"Hi everyone. Thank you. Such a wonderful afternoon and a moment in time we can all be proud of and cherish. Now, if we could pay attention for a minute or so, I want you to listen to this urgent report from WHO."

She switched on the broadcast. The relayed report in discussion with experts in the field, clearly heard and not to be ignored. The picnic in progress fell silent.

"According to Charles Renton, a leading scientist for the World Health Organization, we are less than 40 years away from a food shortage that has serious implications for all people and governments. His comment on food security at the recent UNO conference came with an urgent message. For the first time in human history, food production will be limited on a global scale by the availability of land, water and energy. These shortages could become as politically destabilizing by 2050, as energy issues are today. A monumental challenge of feeding the world lies ahead." The broadcast ended, but Priscilla added further comment.

"This is a battle to be waged. One of many. To bring positive change using advanced weaponry. Tools we have, that our opposition, at this time, do not. Transformational technology, using defence intelligence not greater fire. Let us celebrate today. Tomorrow and every day after, we have work to do. And to each and every one of us 'babies,' Bon Voyage."

Then followed the clink of glasses and voices raised in unison.

"The Ugly Babies!"

Silence, followed by murmurs of discussion between the group, with suggestions of possible plans, strategies and action. Only Brambles could afford to yawn and stretch. Then unexpectedly, Bernard interrupted with an announcement of his own. There were official looking vehicles approaching the house without invitation. Time to button their "cloaks", close ranks and disband. Mission accomplished. The invisible group had successfully drawn local authorities into the field for an opening skirmish.

* * *

The Windstone police report stated, "Following a complaint from an unidentified concerned neighbour, about possible unlawful activity taking place on the premises, an investigative team with officers Chambers and Perkins was dispatched to the Talbot residence on Mulberry Road."

* * *

In counter measure, as part of the minutes for the next Ugly Babies meeting, there were the following notes: "A contingency of police officers with a warrant entered through the front doors of the Talbot residence and immediately searched the rooms before heading into the garden. What they encountered failed to record any worthwhile evidence in their response to an unidentified source claiming disturbance of the peace. The items we left for their consideration can be filed under, successful purple herring hindrance."

* * *

At the Windstone police station, two young police officers, Chambers and Perkins stand at attention, reporting to their superior officer, Sergeant Malcolm Cobb, on their findings of the day before.

"Okay, Perkins. What can you tell me?"

"Not too much to report, sir. It seems like there was some kind of celebration. But no one around when we got there. Therefore, we did not have the opportunity to apprehend or to get statements of what might have taken place."

"Chambers?"

"Some of the food on the plates was still warm."

"Do you think they might have continued their activities at the village pub?"

"We can always check."

"A little late for that now, Perkins. What am I expected to do with a statement wrapped in yesterday's fish and chip paper? Pubs are not night clubs. They close at 11 p.m., clean up, and open the next day for lunch."

"Yes, sir."

"Sergeant, we did find this." Officer Chambers handed Sergeant Cobb a plastic bag containing a battered book.

"*The Teleporter's Handbook?* Did you look inside?"

"No, sir, on account I might be tampering with crucial evidence."

"Hmmm. Leave it with me. Anything else?"

"Something I maybe should mention, and this is going to sound strange, I know."

"Okay, Chambers. What?"

"I did see a large cat floating around the bushes and hovering over the flower beds."

"Give me a moment here. You're telling me you saw a flying cat. With wings or without? Perkins did you also witness this miraculous event?"

"No, sir. I was upstairs checking the bedrooms for evidence of possible substance abuse." Sergeant Cobb gave Officer Chambers a silent stare that demanded further details.

"I didn't say it was flying, Sergeant. It looked more like gliding. Very relaxed and purring, as I remember."

"Should there be further investigation into this incident, do you expect me to record that as a statement for putting in a report and repeating in front of fellow officers and my superiors?"

"I don't know if you would want to do that, sir. I'm just saying that is what I saw."

"You and your wife are about to have your first child. Correct, Officer Chambers?"

"Yes, sir, we are."

"Then I suggest you get some sleep and talk to me the day after tomorrow."

"Yes, sir. Thank you, sir. Will do, sir."

"And not a word to anyone about this. Either of you. Understand? Not anyone!" Chambers and Perkins salute and reply in unison.

"Yes, sir."

"Okay. Dismissed."

After they had left, Sergeant Cobb removed the book from the plastic bag and opened it. Glancing at the index on the first page he read:

The Teleporter's Handbook: Notes and Suggestions. How to combat any of the following:

THE ECOLOGICAL ARMAGEDDON
CLIMATE CHANGE
GENDER EQUALITY AND INJUSTICE
MAN-MADE POLLUTION
FOSSIL FUELS
UNSUSTAINABLE AGRICULTURE
THE ANTIBIOTIC APOCALYPSE
SHRINKING WATER SUPPLIES
FAMINE
DISEASE
OVERPOPULATION

The subjects listed at first appeared to juggle and then rearrange themselves into randomly changing order. Then began to fade and disappear. Sergeant Cobb rubbed his eyes and reached for his glasses. Turning from the first page, he discovered the remaining pages were completely blank. "Just as I suspected, a right bunch of nut-bars," he thought. He wasn't about to make a fool of himself without good reason. That meant he needed hard edged evidence. A flying cat indeed! Without second thought, he was about to toss the book into his desk drawer. The phone rang. Putting the book aside, he answered.

"Hello, Cobb here."After a long day, the voice of his wife on the other end obviously wasn't helping. "Okay. I'm about to leave. Will pick that up on the way home. Be about twenty minutes. Okay. Love you too."

About to pick the book up and take it with him, he decided instead to deal with it in the morning. Then putting on his jacket he headed out of the front door. Two minutes later, with no visible assistance, the book, appearing to levitate, floated towards the front door and exited. The next morning when Sergeant Malcolm Cobb walked back into the office, he noticed the book he had left on his desk the night before was missing. In its place was a crudely drawn felt pen cartoon. It showed an unusual looking baby in a diaper kicking a ball into an open net.

* * *

From those first meetings that tested and baffled the authority of a small English town, a network grew. Reaching across the U.K, Europe and then the globe. At first, the UBO would claim no headquarters with a physical address or offer a political affiliation that could be joined, disputed and challenged. It sought volunteers looking to balance available resources and injustice. Slowly a revolution began to emerge and then take hold. Offering strategy tools that could develop human potential striving for the good of the planet and peaceful co-existence. It addressed nurturing impoverished families, single parents and children, utilizing the harvesting of natural resources, and restructuring the distribution of food supplies and channels of wealth. Encouraging people to form small units with a mandate addressing local problems that would lead to initiating similar changes around the world. Problems formerly caused by greed and prejudice, were now to be challenged and solved, by common sense based on clear objectives. If they had a promo message, it was this.

"Keep your eye out for anyone wearing the lapel pin of a baby only its mother could love. Create the opportunity to address issues that concern you. To achieve real results, it will take working together before ugly babies can grow up to be beautiful adults."

Talbot Residence, Windstone, November 2028

The discovery and excitement the group enjoyed in their early days had been tempered by the challenges of the reality they faced in a world embroiled in continual conflict. Even the cherished memories of their 'invisible' garden party had faded, invisibility having been thwarted by rebel adversaries armed with a wave-reader that detected the shape and outline of the person or object once hidden. What Janet came to understand was that each and every individual of the now much larger organization, at certain times would question and struggle to maintain dedication to their common purpose, and one another. The faith required to move mountains often proved absent, leaving them searching for a reason to believe. Of the original group, Naomi, Cleo, Bentley and Bernard certainly had their own story to tell. And undoubtedly, one day they would tell it. Janet, when looking back, had cause to examine the purpose of what had been accomplished. Currently spending time with Bernard, as a witness and care-giver during his declining health, was proving very difficult for her.

* * *

The comfortable warm living room of the Talbot house. A log sparked and glowed in the fire place. Bernard in a wheel chair with a blanket over his knees. His mind was no longer the instrument of his bidding. The collection of artifacts, photographs, books and souvenirs gathered from his early student studies up to now, surrounded him. Those items established his reputation as a prominent archaeologist to anyone who entered the room. Recently diagnosed with a condition beyond the earlier stages of dementia, his ability to form new memories severely restricted and his self-awareness of that condition fading. Janet's voice called from the kitchen.

"Bernard, dinner will be ready in fifteen minutes."

"Thank you, Priscilla."

Janet smiled and carried on with the food preparation. Bernard often confused her with his sister since she arrived in the Talbot house, at Priscilla's request, to look after him. And Janet was more than happy to be far away from the disruptive events of Los Angeles and the world in turmoil. There was political upheaval taking place almost everywhere. Except it would seem, the English countryside. At least for the time being.

* * *

Across the planet, pockets of warfare erupted continuously. Often without warning. Financed by opposing parties choosing to wage their battle on any turf, other than their own. Targeting a location and attacking unannounced. Then accusing each other without debating, before they retaliated. Ignoring the need, there is a deep spiritual value for a human being when they choose to enter a building to worship, meditate and pray. Whether that be a church, a mosque, a synagogue, a temple or a stone structure built on a high mountain retreat. Voices singing in harmony can be beautiful and the soul can find friendship. But where had all the flowers gone? When will they ever learn? *The fighting and feuding over organized religions is dangerous for each other and the planet!* Puppet leaders, making incendiary speeches full of bluster and rhetoric.

'Surely our community would operate more efficiently by scourging the homeless and unemployed.'

'The time has come to instigate a program for identifying the perpetrators before they can attack and destroy us.'

'Indisputable facts point to a vast number of people of the wrong race and colour and/or religion, who are responsible for our problems.'

Add fish in the ocean with their bellies full of plastic and mercury, being served up in restaurants and constant earthquake warnings. Accompanied by melting ice caps and climate instability. All of these had become part of daily acceptance. Confusion and mayhem. Idiotic solutions peppered and inflamed by constant broadcast updates, social media and reports of misleading victories on the stock exchange. The number of people without food and shelter increasing daily. The future of Mother Earth was approaching TILT. Can you take me to another planet?

"It's your fault or their fault but certainly not OUR fault," echoed around the world.

* * *

Janet was thinking to herself, it was about time Priscilla pulled the rabbit out of the hat once more. Having virtually disappeared, when was she going to surface again? Less than thirty minutes later, the rabbit indeed, popped up. As a result of that, Janet now found herself with a trowel in hand, digging at the base of the cherry tree. She was trying to locate a metal box Priscilla said was buried there for safe-keeping. While digging, Janet ran over that conversation.

"Janet, I want you to listen to me and do not for any reason interrupt the proceedings I am about to set in place. Lives may depend on it."

"Okay. Got it"

"*The Teleporter's Handbook*."

"What about it?"

"The original. Not one of the mock-ups we constructed."

"Then I am not sure I can identify it."

"It is located near the house."

"Then I will find it."

"Good. Here are the instructions. Follow them carefully."

"Go ahead."

"The cherry tree at the back."

"Yes…?"

"The book is inside a small steel box buried at the root of the tree. It can be opened but only with the key I have hidden."

"The key is hidden where?"

"Lower shelf of the bookcase in my bedroom. Taped inside the back cover of T.S. Eliot's *Four Quartets*. Once you have opened the box, take out the *Teleporter's Handbook*. Handle very carefully. The next step is most important. You will need to place a photo of me on the front cover. That is the only way I can gain entry for what I need to accomplish."

"To do what exactly?"

"Get my brother restored."

"How are you proposing to do that?"

"Assuming Bernard will allow me to take over his being, I will attempt to reverse the extreme shrinkage of his cerebral cortex, the hippocampus and reduce the enlarged ventricles."

"You intend to carry out brain surgery by proxy…?

"I will be operating as a robot would be and guided by the photon particles."

"Photon particles?"

"Photons have no mass and travel only at the speed of light. Two particles created at the same time and place rely on quantum entanglement. They effectively have the same existence even when they are separated and changed. So, if one photon changes, the other photon in the separate location changes too. Quantum entanglement."

"Okay, you're losing me here. And for Bernard. What does that accomplish?"

"A relatively normal function of his brain."

"And this handbook will help you, do that?"

"Together, we're hoping to upgrade his present neural faculty and then press his restart button."

"What if that doesn't work?"

"Then we lose my brother a little earlier than expected. And I should probably say my goodbye to you here and now, also."

"Check. Deep breath. What do I do while this is in process?"

"Under no circumstances create disturbance to any changes taking place in the room or to those Bernard may seem to be experiencing. In fact, I suggest you take a nap."

"You're serious!?"

"Given that if, we are successful Bernard will likely not register or understand what has changed or taken place. At best, he will proceed and respond without recalling his prior condition. On no account should you try to explain that to him. I will check in with him tomorrow. See that he gets some rest."

"Copy."

"Let's do this."

Janet had done all that she was asked. Found the book. Located the key. Dug up the box. Opened it, and there it was. *The Teleporter's Handbook*. She removed the book from box and placed it squarely on the desk in Priscilla's bedroom.

Ping! A voice emanating from the book spoke.

"Access ID Verification required."

"I'm about to open you."

"Repeat. Access ID Verification required."

Janet placed the photo of Priscilla squarely on the book cover and small lights began to tango around the room. The book was no longer locked.

Ping!

"Thank you, Janet," said the book.

"Yes. Janet. Thank you."

The voice of Priscilla was unmistakable. She was present in the room.

* * *

Bernard picked up the newest of three scrapbooks full of Priscilla memorabilia and without any undue consideration began tearing and casually dropping a random page into the burning fireplace. He stared blankly as the flames consumed articles, photos and opinions on her research and accomplishments. Scientific breakthroughs pioneering advanced technologies. History dancing in the flames. Janet walked into the room and briefly observed this ceremonial consumption of paper by fire. Bernard seemed to have little awareness of what he was doing. And Janet empathized with his confusion. Where had the efforts to forge new maps into the unknown taken them? And what was being lost? Janet knew without a doubt, there would be many more books written about Priscilla Talbot and her work. And certain of those books might promise a blueprint for personal empowerment of unlimited vistas, possibly enriching your life forever. Those potential changes could be acquired by adopting the encrypted guidelines set down on specific pages. If you were granted access, then came the work required to decode the impenetrable formulae. Together with this footnote. Once you had earned that knowledge by accepting those terms, you would have donated your life force and there would be no turning back.

"Bernard what are you doing?"

"I'm looking for Priscilla."

"She will be in touch soon, I promise."

"When is soon?"

"On my birthday."

"Happy Birthday, Janet."

Bernard resumed depositing another article from his Priscilla scrapbooks into the fireplace. Janet gently removed the remaining scrapbooks for safe-keeping. "Okay, Professor Talbot, time for your dinner." Janet knew there was little she understood or could do about what might happen next.

* * *

It was some time after dinner that Bernard sat up and, for the first time in ages, clearly observed his surroundings and the room. He looked across the table. Janet was quietly napping. She worked way too hard. He stretched his arms and yawned. It was then he noticed. Why was he in a wheelchair? Hmm. Very odd. Without further thought, he stood up, made his way upstairs and went to bed.

* * *

On a sunny afternoon two days later. Janet sat in wonder with her private thoughts of all that had transpired. "This is what life is really about," she thought. "Even in troubled times, keep your faith strong and hold steady in the trust you share with friends, family and each other. And love the planet you're on."

Bernard was up and striding around the living room. Obviously extremely agitated, he was venting to Janet about Priscilla.

"You know when that sister of mine does call. I'm going to give her a piece of my mind."

"You already have."

"What did you just say?"

"I said. Yes, Bernard. You've already made that very clear. In fact, you've talked about little else since you woke up from that long sleep."

"It was a very restful sleep and much needed, I must say. But the point is, and I know we all have busy lives and stuff to do. But she has to understand, the people that are closest to you get stressed when they don't hear from you."

BRIINGG. BRIINGG. BRIINGG.

"Oh, I would place a bet that is her right now," Janet said, about to answer the phone. Bernard beat her to it and picked up.

"Oh, it is you. Buttons what is going on? Yes, I know. You're sorry about that. That's fine. But you really must make more effort. You promise. Okay. I'm just so happy to hear your voice. Most of the time I've been well. Janet has been taking great care of me. No. Those headaches I was having regularly seemed to have disappeared. What about you?"

As Priscilla took the time to update her brother., Janet saw a warm smile taking over the earlier frustration on Bernard's face. "Oh, that will be wonderful. I will let Janet know. She will tell the others I'm sure. Yes, and big hugs for you too."

Bernard ended the call and turned to Janet. He was beaming.

"Priscilla plans to arrive next week for an extended stay. She misses us and needs the break. She asked me to tell you to let the others know. We are going to have a party. A reunion celebration party!"

"Oh, excellent news," said Janet. "Just in time for my birthday."

"Happy Birthday, Janet."

Bernard impulsively pulled Janet onto her feet and together they began an impromptu waltz. With the evening sun shining through the bay windows of the beautiful old country house, Bernard and Janet sailed around the room like two swans on a lake.

* * *

Following Priscilla's explicit instructions, Janet was to return the book, in the steel box, back under the tree. She took the trowel and dug a space deep around the earth covering the roots. There it was done. Ping! *The Teleporter's Handbook* closed. Safely locked inside. The box returned to its home. She patted the surrounding soil back into place. The cherry tree stood where it had always stood. Only…as Janet stood back from the trunk of the tree, blossoms began springing on the branches. Big beautiful flowers sending their sweet aroma into the warm evening air. For a moment Janet thought she may have been dreaming but there was no mistaking what she heard the breeze whisper; "There is a voice that doesn't use words. Listen."

Notes from The Front (2): Syria, 2039

U.B.O Base, Zone 7. Teleportation of food and support materials successfully completed from Zone 3 Keflavik, Iceland to Zone 5, Rojava, Syria. One shipment has apparently been untraceable since dispatch, possibly intercepted by cyber insurgents. We are posting this as a surveillance interference alert. Guaranteed safe passage for teleport routes must be secured. Codes should be reset and protected. Suggest using mind-wave transmissions until completed for key data exchange to avoid digital capture. The tanks and drones still roam the territories they once ruled but are now only policing the wasteland of their own making. There is no sign of innovation or restoration. Mother Earth has been ravaged, shaken and dishevelled. The shock tremors constantly reverberating. Her recovery, if possible, will require telepathic intelligence and awareness to keep the human cockroaches from feasting on what remains. And so, our concerted effort to train suitable applicants must continue. Officers Cleo and Bentley delivered four units of recently recruited 'ugly babies' to designated 'nurseries' in the past month. All have been approved after passing their sensory monitoring potential. We are expecting to advance and transfer forty percent of them into pre-operational status within three months. Those not ready to enter this stage can be employed as field workers in secured global locations. We estimate, of the forty percent, twenty-seven percent will advance to secure functional status within six months. If so, they will be armed with defence and engagement shields after appropriate training* (see note below). Once approved and stable on their own two feet, 'babies' can be classified within their adopted family as adults and qualified to train new recruits. Our army of ugly babies has grown. We are far larger, stronger, better equipped and committed, more than ever, to our cause. Forecasting no ascendancy for one side or the other. Victory in the face of irrevocable damage, will at best, offer a muted celebration. Much work still needs to be done.

**Invisibility cloaking: Concern increases that this may no longer be a reliable 'adopt and advance' strategy until upgraded against detection. In some zones it has become recognised and disarmed by opposition units using wave-sound lasers. Operational Programs Director Naomi has my fully detailed report. Water shortages are approaching Day Zero in many locations around the world. Peace.*

(2)
TANK AND COCO

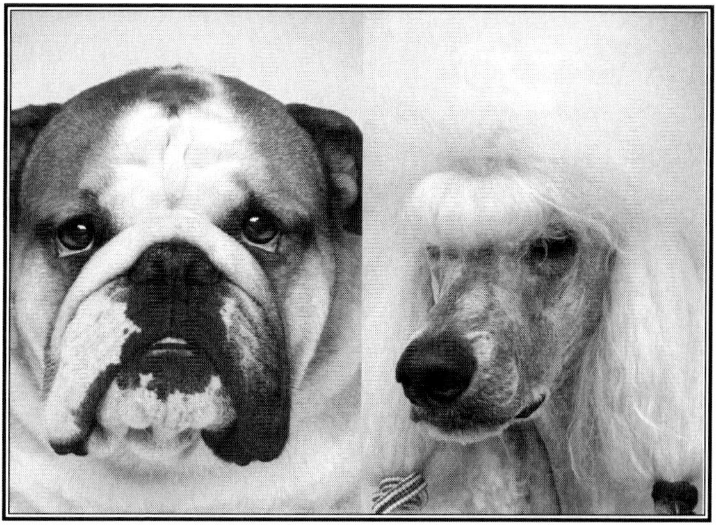

Tank and Coco were the last two standing. Yolanda, the cup-size yappy Chihuahua had taken herself out of the running. The child she had bitten was now being tended to and the judges were busy consoling the girl's mother. Tank looked at Coco and sniffed.

"It doesn't surprise me in the least. Sticking a bunch of pearls and a pink tutu on a dog that weighs more than the animal itself! If you can call that a dog. Ha! What were they thinking? The pressure was too much. Anyway, it was a no brainer who the finalists would be."

Tank, the British bulldog, was resolute in trying to get the attention of the snobby French poodle with the coiffed hair and curled eyelashes, standing next to him. He had an agenda and did not intend to end up second best. For sure he would have considered giving her a tumble if the right circumstances presented themselves. She did have nice legs and a certain way of scratching her backside. And those curls and fancy ribbons she displayed were appealing. Meanwhile, Coco was having a teeny bit of trouble with the third toenail of her left front paw. Lifting that leg and checking the nail, she fluttered her blue eyes behind huge lashes. No way was she going to let on that a toenail could be a problem in the competition. And this ignorant lout standing next to her? Well, he was going to have to get on board with finishing as runner-up.

"Revolution," said Coco, making little or no sense, as she often did when trying to be seductive. "Revolution builds slowly, at first it smoulders and then suddenly explodes."

Tank, refusing to be deterred, shook his ear. He had no idea what this uppity poodle was talking about. He was hoping to find a tactic to undermine the obvious advantage of height and poise his opponent had. An overture of friendly conversation, might give him even a hint of how this poodle thinks.

"It's impossible to win these days unless you are a pure bred. First rate lineage and the papers to prove it."

"Difficile convenu mais pas impossible." Coco insisted.

Oh boy, this wasn't going to be easy. Tank would have to cope, not only with her aloof attitude but *also* his own dismal lack of 'parlez-vous francais'. Never mind, he knew a thing or two about the strategy of doing battle.

"A beautiful smile can accomplish a lot" Coco commented in her heavily accented English.

"Maybe; but these days you don't get rewarded just because you have a nice smile." said Tank, "You need a lot more than that."

Coco, flashed her immaculate pearly whites, silently thinking; "Cela aiderait si vous aviez des dents decentes." ('it would help if you had decent teeth').

Tank, ignoring the smile, continued; "I know what these dog shows are all about. Do you?"

"Je fais certainment! The best dog wins?"

"If only it were that simple"

"Je te trouve is amusant".

"If you think i'm only here to amuse you, then excuse me for talking," said Tank. "Excuse me!"

"Si amusant! You are obviously a pro-Brexit dog if ever I met one."

"What did you just say!"

"I said, 'you are obviously a pro-Brexit dog. Et je troupe ca tres amusant."

"What is that supposed to mean!"

Tank was obviously riled. And Coco liked it that way.

"Avez vous un problème pour comprendre pro-Brexit?"

"Me, have a problem? Why would I have a problem? I am the genuine article. Most of what you see around here are accidental couplings.

A quick shag in the park when the owner is not looking. And Voila! Excuse my poor French. But that's all it takes. Mutts. Random bred mutts. Fated to lead undisciplined lives on a rope leash. Or no leash at all. Perish the thought. Outrageous!"

"Ne te fache pas! Les Brittaniques sort tres bons pour etre snobs"

Coco had obviously hit a nerve and Tank was always ready for a tussle.

"If only they knew who they were dealing with before their nose went up in the air. Who do they think they are kidding? Nobody but themselves. That's for sure."

Coco preened her scented curls, content to have Tank rant as much as he wanted. His breath was filling the air between them and Coco catching a whiff of it, recoiled.

"Mauvaise hygeine" her nose told her. Bad diet. Equals bad teeth. Tel puant. "Comment plus évident pourriez vous être. Le paradis nous aide! C'est grotesque". No need for her to say a word. Let Tank sink his own boat. He seemed eager to oblige.

Tank continued trying to steer their conversation, "I've been keeping a close eye on what is going on around here since I arrived. There's nobody here you could call a contender. You have nothing to worry about." Coco countered with a dismissive remark. "Why would I be worried?"

"History and family background," said Tank. "That's what matters. You will not find any self -respecting bulldog parading around for a silver cup and a medal. Competing with a pack of mongrels? Not interested."

"You're not interested in the prizes?" Coco said, playing along.

"Oh prizes. Are you kidding. I have a cabinet full of trophies and ribbons as long as your eyelashes. That's what I keep saying. Family history. That's what it's all about. Pedigree. You of course, wouldn't know how much that counts on occasions like these."

"Oh," said Coco "How fascinating. That's an interesting statement to make. Tell me more before they announce the winner."

"Right. Heritage matters. My family can trace a prestigious line of owners. Among them," Tank took a deep breath. "William.... ."

"William.?" said Coco

"That's right."

"William....William Shakespeare?"

"No," said Tank a little miffed.

"Tell...? William Tell?"

"Nah nah," said Tank clenching his teeth and shaking his head.

"William of Orange?

"Nope."

"William The Conqueror?"

"We kicked him back to Normandy," gloated Tank.

"William Wyler?" said Coco somewhat ruffled.

"Movie director! Ha!" Tank was very much enjoying this game.

"William Archibald the first dean of Canterbury Cathedral?" ventured Coco, quite aware she was watering the wrong tree.

"No. No." Tank growled resolutely.

"It must be William Cody. Buffalo Bill."

"Nope."

"Wild Bill Hickok?".

"Not even close."

"Oh. Oh. I know. The guy who owns the chocolate factory. Wonka. William Wonka." Coco raised her head and one paw, as if celebrating her triumph.

"Even further off the mark."

"I give up," Coco said, disinterested.

Savouring the moment, Tank the bulldog took his time.

"William," he said slowly, "Wordsworth."

"WILLIAM WORDSWORTH!" yelped Coco. "Ha. Ha! Ha!!"

"Yep the one and only," said Tank proudly. "Me and mine are poet's dogs."

"Is that a fact?" Coco was unimpressed.

"Yep. That's a fact."

"Well," said Coco. "That is nothing to wag your tail about. Even if you had one. I mean clouds? *Mon dieu!* Tell me, what is so very special about poems that go on and on about clouds. Give me a little Rimbaud, Absinthe and Cognac. Emile Zola. *Merci beaucoup!*" Tank was very aware of the slight to his pedigree and quick to retaliate.

"We are such a pure strain. There are very few dogs who can say that. Take your breed. Rumour has it you were cross bred with an Hungarian water dog. And to note, your tail is a pompon!. Pooh. Why? It allowed hunters to see you and save you from drowning if you got in over your head. Which brings me to the point. Maybe we pure bred English bulldogs don't hang out with just any canine. However, we are always very polite if treated with respect. So just keep your paws from crossing over the line. You understand?"

"No, I don't, actually," said Coco rudely.

"Well take you for instance," said Tank. "You and yours are bred to poise, prance and gossip. Decked out with ribbons and curls. Whereas, me and mine establish ourselves in majestic homes nurturing habits that continue for generations. You and yours? You act like second rate celebrities. We are homebodies that look to our master for our upkeep and maintenance by keeping watch and providing protection. It's about being good company on a nice long walk, feeling the green grass of Hampstead Heath underneath your paws. You and yours? Maybe you offer a certain entertainment value. Like a music hall act. Me and mine, earn our reputation from solid service.

Coco was not going to allow this watery eyed overweight pooch to get away with that remark. Baring her teeth and giving Tank the regal eye, she exclaimed:

"Marie Antionette was no music hall act. She was the last queen of France. *Mettez ça dans votre pipe et fumezle! Des nudges. Hah!* "

Tank felt the studded collar tighten around his neck. If she wanted a scuffle. Okay, she would get more than she bargained for.

"Eat cake. You mutt" he snarled.

"Yes, talking of mutts," said Coco, "Before you go jumping around high horses. Every dog has the right to have one. Remember that."

"The right to have one? Have what?" said Tank puzzled.

"You'll find out soon enough," said Coco. "You and yours have had yours. Me and mine are about to have ours."

"Are we talking popularity here?" said Tank. "On your bike! You see old Fritz over there, the dachshund with the monocle? He and his predecessors have been grand prize winners. Look at him now. He's so low to the ground he's developed a rug rash from being dragged over fake turf carpet. Any dog who has been around long enough, knows it. You walk up and down, then stand on these dumb platforms getting judged. Why try to teach an old dog new tricks that a monkey does far better. In the end, for all its worth you might get an extra biscuit thrown to you on a cold kitchen floor. Maybe, an extra pat and 'What a good dog you are.' And you know why that is happening to us.? I'll tell you why. It's because they are having more and more of these floor shows to make profit for the greedy pet food corporations!" Tank was beginning to foam at the mouth. Tugging at his leash. "Promoting fancy breeds and freak mutations. Just so they can sell more tasteless food crammed with sawdust. Junk food for us who live here and fought for this country. *Feeding the real chunks of juicy chicken and beef in that delicious gravy* *TO FOREIGN MONGRELS AND THEIR LIKE! WE BRITISH BULLDOGS MUST UNITE! REVOLUTION!!"*

At this point, it can be said, Tank was absolutely 'barking mad'. Coco smiled sympathetically. They knew all about revolutions where she came from and where had that got them? This was a dog show competition and she was here to win. She sensed her mission was about to be accomplished. Tank was now howling at the top of his voice and every dog in the hall turned around and stared at him. He tried to cover his tirade in as peaceful a way as possible. He even tried smiling. But it was too late. The judges were approaching them. Everything stopped. Eyes checking each other out. Dog checking dog. Man checking dogs. Woman checking dogs. Man checking woman. Woman checking man. Dogs checking judges. Any moment now *The Royal Ruffs Best in Show*, was about to be announced. The man held the Silver Cup, the woman held the bright shiny medal attached to the myriad of red white and blue silk ribbons. An assistant held the diploma for runner up prize winner. Tank and Coco knew the drill. Both were in it to win first place prize. The judges conferred with the sponsors and the sponsors were clearly not happy with the outburst Tank had demonstrated. Under their close scrutiny, Tank began to slobber uncontrollably. The drips from his jaw and lips began to form a small pool beneath his chin and fell to the floor. It was enough. A decision had been made. The man with the cup told the woman with the medallion, and they both made a mention to the assistant with the diplomas. He then whispered to their owners and the sponsors. That day Tank learned that contrary to popular folklore, a bark can be a lot worse than a bite. And also, it doesn't pay to offend other breeds whatever country they're from, even if you think they are mutts. Especially French poodles. As the man with the diploma gave Tank the ribbon for second place, he heard Coco whisper,

"*Monsieur Tank, vous avez un point. Cependant, bien due* pedigree matters, but good teeth and a brilliant hairdresser can win the day. *Le charme conquiert tout!*"

Tank swore that was the moment he heard a poodle chuckle for the first time. Coco gave a slight shift of her head as the winner medal with silk ribbon fell about her neck. The applause in the hall was tumultuous. Tank growled in Coco's ear.

"This dog show is not over."

The next day. A small photo of Coco with the winner ribbon around her neck, posing next to the shiny cup. But the bigger headline read, "*Ruckus at Royal Ruffs Dog Show. Every Dog Has Its Day?* The news article that followed, informed readers: "*Finale ends in protest*. *Animal activists storm arena. Chihuahua bites child. Bulldog attacks judge.*"

(3)
A TALL LEPRECHAUN TALE

Leprechauns being just wee folk a few inches in height? Larry chuckled to himself. Who made up such nonsense!? He was born from the lineage of the Tuatha de Danann, an ancient race of giant creatures, elves and goblins. Many of them taller than the average person of today. So, Larry knew differently. He stood just short of six feet on every day of the year but one. Also, contrary to what most people believe, leprechauns are not just mythical fairy folk in stories. They actually exist. And furthermore, their colour of preference in costume and origin is blue, not green. Green having been adopted as a camouflage to avoid detection in their preferred habitat of woodlands, gardens, caves, and long grass. These misnomers enabled them to hide-in-plain-sight supported by numerous old wives' tales, claiming they were from the Emerald Isle, always dressed in green, had red beards and cherished the shamrock, which had three leaves representing faith, hope, and love. Or as some would have it, the holy trinity. A four-leaf clover, if you could find one, made you lucky. That being said, you might pick ten thousand shamrocks before you found one of those. Though Larry himself, would vouch to have discovered clovers that had five leaves. Whether that be true and matters, readers can decide for themselves. What Larry did often ponder was, did Brigid his wife suspect he was a leprechaun? She had never let on to him if she did. And on the eve of every St. Patrick's Day he would tuck their children Shawn and April into bed, kiss them on the forehead and whisper.

"Now don't you be harming the leprechauns if you catch one. And a Happy St. Patrick's Day to ya!"

Then Larry would disappear for twenty four hours saying he was off to play in a golf tournament for a good cause. It was the only night of the year he was away from his family. The truth be told, usually on any given March 17th you would be almost certain to find Larry in a hidden underground cave underneath the garden shed. Soundproof and built for privacy many years ago. It was a very safe and comfortable spot to hang out undisturbed. There he would sit with a set of golf clubs and irons, enjoying a Guinness along with the occasional shot of Jameson whiskey, watching golf tournaments on his iPad. While Brigid and the kids would carry out their own plans and head into town with friends for the festivities. This allowed Larry to be alone for the day, doing what leprechauns were born to do. Dream of acquiring gold. And also, planning a way to escape should they be caught. And here are some other lesser known facts. Being a leprechaun on St. Patrick's Day meant even the ordinary wee leprechaun doubled in size and could walk around in costume for 24 hours incognito. That meant, tomorrow, Larry was going to be almost twelve feet tall, wearing a bright blue jerkin, leprechaun hat and gold buckled shoes. And there was one other very important matter for consideration. He was planning to rob the bank.

With these thoughts running around his head, Larry sat ruminating what he would do with the money. He had ambitions to go into politics. Possibly, he might become the first leprechaun to serve as mayor? And like Robin Hood, after robbing the rich, he would give to the poor. But what if they caught him? He knew people set traps to catch leprechauns with a trail of worthless gold coins and fake lucky clovers. But being an authentic leprechaun such as he was, that was unlikely to fool him. He was too large for any trap set. Nevertheless, should he be caught, he speculated what three wishes would he be obliged to grant? It is important to keep in mind once a leprechaun is captured, he is bound to tell the truth. That was the nature of his being. Except if you took your eye off him for one second then he could make himself disappear. POOF! Just like that! For that reason alone, you can always be sure a leprechaun will be thinking one step ahead.

* * *

Recalling his humble beginnings as an apprentice cobbler in County Clare, where he quickly became known for excellent workmanship at a young age. Larry specialized in mending just one shoe only and cleaning the shiny gold buckle. There had been more than one instance when the shoe having been fixed, would be returned to the owner with the original buckle missing. And it is natural to suppose that Larry, might have stashed them somewhere. That hiding place being a very large pot, and that pot being, as you might have guessed, located at the end of his parent's property. Since that time, Larry had met and married his beautiful wife Brigid, had two children, Shawn and April, and together as a loving family, they had left Ireland years ago. None of whom were leprechauns except himself. But soon after settling in a township near Portland, Oregon, he and Brigid opened a Celtic gift shop. At first, they would spend most of their time in the back room and kitchen making souvenirs for tourists. Miniature shoe necklaces and earrings. Money boxes. Hats and buckle belts. Shamrocks of all sizes. Leprechaun good luck trinkets and such. The two children were kept busy, cutting green construction paper widthwise, to form two long rectangles and then with a black marker, drawing a belt on the newly cut pieces. Sometime later, Larry and his wife sold the business and bought the nice family house that had now become their home. Brigid loved her garden and for the time being everyone was relatively content. But leprechauns get restless and it's their nature to create mischief. And what Larry was planning was not the stealing of a shoe buckle or two. Robbing a bank was far more than mischievous. Those wishes he would have to grant, if captured, troubled him. You could always count one of the wishes would be to do with money, winning the lottery or similar. But what about the other two? Thoughts such as those, keep the mind of a leprechaun busy. The second wish might involve property or if the individual was really smart, good health for themselves and their family. Then there was the wish of meeting the right person to spend the rest of their life with. Good luck with that one, was Larry's opinion. He had certainly been a lucky leprechaun in that regard. Brigid was a true beauty in every respect. And let us not forget what was written in the leprechaun book of proper conduct. Once three wishes are granted, a leprechaun is off the hook and free to go. The receiver had to accept what they had wished for. What had been written for the ages and well known in the recorded history of magical folk, was this. The special skill of the leprechaun was to have their captor make a wish and then have that person wish they hadn't wished it. And that was the thing about wishes in general. They seldom turned out to deliver what you thought, in the way you might have imagined. Still and all, if he was captured it was better to be thinking how he could escape and what it might cost him before he did so. He needed to prepare for the transformation that was going to be his reality for the next 24 hours. Larry took a deep breath and sang a traditional Irish song of his ancestors. Standing naked in front of the mirror he saw himself grow and expand. Almost twelve feet tall. Okay, now he was ready to dress for the occasion. Midnight blue jerkin and pants, gold buckle shoes and leprechaun hat. Without a weapon, other than his giant stature and outstanding attire, Larry set out to rob the bank.

* * *

March 18. The day after St. Patrick's. The kids were playing outside. Brigid was preparing an early dinner and expecting Larry to arrive back home from his golf tournament at any moment. Glancing out of the kitchen window she observed the vibrant colours and arrangements in her beloved garden.

"It must be a blessing to have your own personal leprechaun, she thought. "Making everything in the garden grow greener. 'Tis surely plants and flowers do appreciate the company." Brigid considered Larry to be a magical man for sure. The clock on the stove alarm interrupted her thoughts, suggesting the scones were ready. Brigid opened the oven door and as she put the fresh baked scones on top of the stove to cool, Larry's voice announced,

"I'm home, darling." Larry walked into the living room, put down his golf bags and kissed her on the cheek. "Sorry I'm late," said Larry. "The Volvo refused to start when I turned the ignition this morning. Then I had to drop Freddy off."

"How did the game go?"

"Oh, much the same as usual. Lots of dirty jokes, cursing and missed putts. Hmmm. Smells good. What are we having for dinner?"

"Lamb chops. potatoes and brussel sprouts."

"Sounds delicious."

"Lend me a hand with the potatoes"

"Where are the kids?"

"Out in the garden looking for leprechauns."

"Not to disappoint them but this being the day after St Patrick's, I'm sure those wee folk are having a quiet nap and sleeping it off."

"Napping or not, the kids are convinced we have one living in the hyacinths."

Larry, avoiding adding further comment, filled the saucepan with water from the tap.

"Did anyone call today?"

"Helen McJarvis showing off again about her darling daughter Celia."

"Who has darling Celia been impressing of late pray tell, besides ourselves?"

"Darling Celia, is heading to Tokyo next month, learning how to make 'authentic sushi', is what Helen would have me believing."

"Authentic is it.? From what I recall the lovely Celia could barely peel a carrot. Let's hope those people over there understand what that young lady goes rattling on about when she opens her mouth. Because 'tis more than often, I cannot,"

As Larry was putting the saucepan on the stove, he absently began whistling, 'Let me call you sweetheart', changing the words in his head to 'Leprechaun your sweetheart.' Brigid looked out of the window. She was content now Larry was home. The smell of food. A warm and cozy kitchen. The sky held a warm evening sun that fell across trees, over the rooftops, visiting the peaceful street they lived on, brushing the faces of the people who said hello, mellowing the passing of time.

"Where does past time go?" Brigid said aloud without thinking.

"What would you be bothering your head with that for?"

"It's a wonder is what it is. Sometimes it makes us wait and then takes off with no regard for what the clock might have us be doing with it."

"No good worrying about time. As soon as you're not looking, off it flies."

"Was Fergus playing today?"

"Oh no, Fergus has no time for hitting a little white ball from one hole to the next. He's far too busy spinning in circles. And his wife helping him do it. Weaving the same old yarn."

"What does that mean?"

"It's as though he can barely detect the nose on his face. Back and forth on the deck of an imaginary ship, he goes running, as if it was about to go up in flames. And just as he's about getting the fire under control, she's up and starting another one with her hot tongue."

"Better quarreling with somebody else's head than arguing with your own."

"I suppose that be true."

"Boiled or mashed?"

"I fancy them mashed with lots of butter."

"And what did my darlin' wife do on St. Patrick's Day?"

"Dropped the kids off to school. Went to the mall and met Maureen for coffee. Oh, and Josie Collopy joined us."

"And what did you ladies get to talking about?'

"It being St. Patrick's Day we sat around and told some tales we'd heard as kids."

"And is Josie Collopy still insisting it was St Patrick who rid the snakes from Ireland when there never was one snake living there?"

"No, but she told us a fine leprechaun story."

"And what would that be"

"Her boyfriend Andrew, is a geologist and some time back, he went on a field trip to County Wicklow. Off to the old country digging up old rocks. Which, if it is to be believed, had a gold rush there."

"A gold rush in county Wicklow?"

"More than two hundred years ago. So I was told."

"Might be worth a visit someday."

"Not much gold left to be found nowadays. And to be sure, if there was, the government owns all of it, you might ever dig up."

"Well that would be a wasted trip, then."

"County Wicklow is a beautiful place."

'True enough. What has that to do with the story Josie Collopy told you?"

"It isn't the end of it by far."

"Okay then rather me watching the potatoes boil, let me hear it."

Larry settled in for what he knew was going to be a cock and bull tale, if Josie Collopy had been part of the telling. Brigid continued; "While Andrew was there in County Wicklow, he picked up a souvenir from the local gift shop. A tin replica of a golden snuffbox said to have been made after melting down the largest nugget of gold ever found in Ireland. And this golden snuff box had been given to King George the Third of England as a gift."

"That would be the English robbing the Irish, once again. Nothing new in that."

"Let us not forget though, he was the mad king they say gave away America. Foaming at the mouth and spewing nonsense in buckets. A real certifiable one."

"They're all a little crazy over there as well we know it."

"That might be true, but might it have been the gold snuff box that did it?"

"Did what?"

"Made that king bonkers."

"You got me following the tale now, so go ahead."

"As Andrew tells it, even this cheap tin replica of the real gold snuff box caused all manner of strange events to take place, especially on or around St Patrick's Day."

"What kind of strange events?"

"Andrew swore a leprechaun used it as a hiding place."

"And what will you be telling me next?"

"Andrew happened to mention it to Paddy, a friend of his, who laughed in his face when he heard it. And Andrew bet Paddy a hundred dollars, he would not be laughing if he lived with that tin snuff box for a week."

"What did Paddy do?"

"He took the bet."

"Only a fool wouldn't."

"Will you be saying that after you hear what took place?"

"Okay Brigid I'm listening."

"Paddy had been out having a few drinks with his friends and was relaxing watching the tele late at night, when this tin snuff box on a nearby table, began sending out a beam of gold light."

"Did he look inside the box?"

"No, he figured it was he himself drunk and needed to get some shut eye."

"And that be the end of it?"

"Oh no. It certainly wasn't. The very next moment, the channel changed for no reason at all and a little man with curly red hair, a big grin, eyes like stars and pointed ears appeared on screen. And this wee creature less than a foot tall, jumped out of the TV set down onto the carpet, climbed up Paddy's trousers, grabbed him by the scruff of his sweater and bit Paddy on the nose. Then he vanished back into the television set. The doctor who examined the bite on the Paddy's nose said, it could have been done by a leprechaun for all he knew, because in all his years of practise that mark was unlike anything he had ever seen before."

"Would it be funny cartoons that this Paddy was watching at the time?"

"Maybe. But Josie Collopy also told us something else. That television has not worked one day properly since then."

"Well, expecting me believe that to be true would be feeding biscuits to a bear."

"It does sound a little far-fetched for sure."

"And what happened to the tin snuff box?"

"Paddy buried it in the garden of his neighbour, he has a grievance with. And then he gave Andrew the hundred dollars for the bet he'd lost."

"Well that's a tall one and it took care of the time for boiling the potatoes".

"And I have an even better one than that."

"Oh, you have a better one than that, do you?"

"And this one happened right here yesterday. Downtown on St Patrick's Day itself. Fit to curl your toes."

"Well don't keep me wondering."

"While you were out golfing yesterday. Did you not manage to catch the news?"

"The news?"

"The bank robbery downtown. While everybody was at the park dancing and enjoying the celebrations, somebody dressed as a leprechaun, robbed the bank."

"A leprechaun robbed the bank! 'Tis my leg you are pulling!

"Dressed in a blue jerkin, gold buckle shoes and a leprechaun hat when he did it."

"And not even wearing the green! What kind of leprechaun would that be?"

"A giant one he was too. Almost twelve feet tall by all accounts."

"Maybe it was St Patrick himself, short on funds and needing some coin."

"It's all anyone is talking about."

"That story tops the lot. As mad as a box of frogs, that one is for sure."

"Well it is a fact."

"It begs the question whether what we believe about leprechauns to be true or not?"

"That I would never say, Larry. 'Tis almost blasphemous."

"Then I would like to have captured that one and see what wishes he would grant us before we set him free."

Larry wondered to himself, and not for the first time, Brigid was closer to the truth than she knew. Or, maybe closer than she cared to admit to him?

* * *

Dinner was ready and on the table. The kids said hello to their dad but wanted to play in the garden. They were intent on capturing a leprechaun and claimed they had seen one in the shadow of the plants.

"Brigid darling, pass me the Brussel sprouts."

When Brigid heard Larry speak her name it was like the sound of musical bells. However, she was not fooled for a second. He had been up to something while he was away. But she knew better than to ask questions. She recalled the rhyme she had learned as a child. The answer could only be revealed behind another question. And always ended up in a riddle:

How much pressure can a leprechaun take
It really depends on the gold he can make.
How much does he measure from his head to the floor?
It always depends on the height of the door...

It was at times like these she knew why she loved him so much. And was reminded of an old story she had once read, where a flower and a leprechaun promised to love and shelter each other as long as they both shall live. And when God looked down and saw this, he asked them both, what they needed most for what they lacked. The leprechaun asked for a pot of gold and a rainbow and the flower asked for a garden. Larry and Brigid had been granted both.

***

The next day Larry had gone to get the car checked out for an ignition problem. Brigid was enjoying a quiet moment making her shopping list. She heard the car in the driveway. It sounded like the Volvo was running just fine. Larry was back.

"It's fixed, and we can go and fetch groceries any time you're ready."

"The kids will probably want to come with us."

"Yes, I said I would be bringing them a present back after my golf game. And didn't have the chance to pick anything up. We can do that when we are downtown."

"Where are they?"

"They're outside playing. Come to think of they've been unusually quiet."

"That could spell trouble for us." There was a noise from the garden, Shawn and April were arguing over something as a brother and sister are wont to do. Suddenly the relative peace and quiet of the kitchen was disrupted as they came rushing into the house.

"Look what we found."

"Look!" Shawn and April were clutching large handfuls of board game money and waving it in the air.

"We bet there's a lot more of this hidden too."

"Heaven to help us. Where did you get that money?"

"We captured a leprechaun."

"And made him promise us money."

"How did you manage to do that?"

"He gave us three wishes to set him free."

"Money, my guess was only one of them."

"Yes it was", the kids yelled in unison.

"What about the other two?"

"Yes, what were the other two?"

"April made him promise he would stay and live with us forever."

"Then Shawn told him he must never get into trouble with police."

"And then what?"

"And then the leprechaun pointed to the big pot at the back of the garden shed."

"…and told us never even try to open the large green canvas bag inside the pot."

"… because what was in it would disappear and we would never see him again."

"….and it had a big lock on it…."

"…so, we couldn't if we wanted to."

"But the leprechaun pointed to the sky and said if we were truly lucky we would surely see a pig fly."

"And did you?"

"Yes, a big blue one with orange ears."

"…and then the leprechaun vanished."

"I said to never take your eye of a leprechaun for a second." accused Shawn.

"It was not my doing." April protested.

"Now, who will believe us?" Shawn said.

"Ah, but this does sound like typical leprechaun behaviour," said Larry. "They get up to playing tricks on you. And this is very important. Not even a whisper about this to another soul. Or the leprechaun may never come back."

"What your father tells you is true enough. Now hurry up. Give your Da the money. Get your coats. We're heading to the shops downtown." Shawn and April handed over the monopoly money and ran off to get their coats.

"They enjoy getting up to mischief."

"Like their father."

"And telling a story or two."

"A healthy imagination. 'Tis the privilege of children."

"It would appear we have a leprechaun living with us."

"Indeed, it would. Say no more."

(4)
GOD BLESS MICHAEL CAINE

There was an undeniable buzz in the room. Rona Cole knew she had nailed the audition. Niels Warren, the director was beaming. The writer too. Even Carl, the camera person was enthused. Sue Chambers, the casting director, nodding her approval, spoke.

"Rona, we are unlikely to see a better reading for this role. Or any other for that matter. We do have a few auditions to carry out and before we wrap this with a decision. Let me just add, a big thank you for coming in today. There is one last question Niels, our director, has for you."

"Niels?"

"Rona. Excellent work. Now in a simple statement to the camera, let us know what it would mean for you to get this role. And be truthful,"

Sue Chambers added,

"And darling, we don't need you to say you would knock boots with Santa Claus or anyone we might know."

Some nervous laughter filled the room before Rona took a deep breath and addressed the lens. "I want the part in this movie so much you could kill me on camera, if it made it a better film."

Silence followed before Sue Chambers looking to the other people in the room, spoke.

"Wow! That could not have been more compelling."

Niels Warren adjusted his sunshades and stood up. "Thank you, Rona. You will be hearing from us shortly."

The next day Rona was hanging by the phone when it rang. She picked it up.

"Rona darling, Zelda here. What you did in that room yesterday knocked them out."

"It felt so right. I knew I aced it!"

"One little hitch and then we get a contract signed."

"A hitch?"

"Yes. Nothing to worry about."

"Nothing always means something, Zelda. Give me what you know."

"Niels is interested in having you come back to discuss the role and further explore something you stated on camera for them. Including other options, you may be interested in pursuing."

"Options?"

"You know how they talk. Around in circles dangling carrots."

"Tell me Zelda. Does that mean I'm currently a donkey about to turn into a thoroughbred racehorse? I did notice by the way, Niels cracking his knuckles. Does he do that in auditions generally?"

"He was cracking his knuckles when you spoke to him!?"

"On both hands."

"Awesome. Okay, here's what I can tell you. They wanted to see you tomorrow but I said the earliest would be Friday afternoon. Same place, 2:30. You're a star!"

* * *

It was the afternoon of the callback. Rona walked into the same room. Something didn't feel right. What had changed? The lighting? The colour of the walls? Had someone spiked her Americano? Definitely a charged tension in the air. However, she recognized Niels Warren, and there was another man sitting next to Niels who Rona had yet to meet. He stood up and greeted her.

"Pardon me for not shaking hands. It's the flu season, and I've got a busy schedule. Chuck Proust."

Niels added, "Chuck is a producer. A very successful producer, I might add."

"Okay, Niels, no need to pour it on too thick here."

"Chuck even your modesty is respected and admired."

"Let me start out by saying this, and then we can move on to the reason we called you in. We are most excited by the prospect of working with you."

"Obviously," confirmed Niels. Somewhat like a casual improvisation with an underlying plot, Rona could feel the rhythm of their pitch ramp up like a finely tuned machine. With their comments building and often overlapping, Rona felt like she was a spectator at a professional tennis match. Niels led off with a compliment.

"First, on the project you auditioned for yesterday. It has already been said, but I would personally like to say it again, for the people in the room. You nailed it."

"Thank you."

"However, there could be a problem with the production money not being available until a future date. It is not a choice we have made, but one that has been made for us."

"And that means?"

"Though we may not have the go ahead on the project you auditioned for, what you did in the room yesterday suggested an exciting alternative." Chuck picked it up.

"...and we feel you should very much be part of what we are visualizing."

"Which is?"

"A project in mind that inadvertently or otherwise was inspired by you."

"A project I inspired?" Rona was understandably flattered. Serving like it was a set point, Niels zeroed in.

"Often these days, as you may be aware, there is more money in television than in movies. You made a statement that caused me to call Chuck in Los Angeles and send him the video clip."

"...only to find out I was on vacation in the Virgin Islands..."

"Richard Branson, a friend of Chuck's, owns the island..."

"Niels will you stop that!"

The banter continued with Rona seeking clarity. She wondered what the hell was going on here. Were they for real? Fuelled by enthusiasm, Niels continued.

"What Chuck is proposing is a reality television series based on individuals willing to jump off various location points. Bridges, office towers, apartment buildings. Famous landmarks. Cliffs and mountains. What would we call it?"

Chuck waved answering the question aside, answering; "Something we can talk about later."

Niels picked up the pitch once more,…"but it would involve…travel to some exotic locations all over the world."

"Are you serious?"

Chuck nodded, "Yes. We would feature a bio profile on the jumper of the week, family history, photographs, school friends, personal dreams and ambitions. Tracking their history from when they were born, through growing up until…Ba- Boom. Name in headlights!"

It was Niels turn to take over with Chuck responding.

"Picture this. An establishing shot. And then we zoom in for a final statement and zoom out as they jump. But a tight close-up on that very poignant moment they do."

"Absolutely."

"And featuring their favourite songs in the background."

Rona stopped them at this point. She had a question or three that needed answering.

"And what do you think makes someone crazy enough to do this. What if they actually die?"

"Unlikely but… an outside possibility," said Chuck

"People do insane things every day, check out the internet," said Niels.

"After the initial pilot, you would be absolved from any responsibility that involved their decision." Chuck quickly added.

"A contract agreement signed by them beforehand."

"And remember the 'you' would now be 'us, including *you*."

"Absolving us and you…from any kind of legal responsibility."

"We have an excellent team of lawyers in place." Chuck assured her.

"Heaven knows we do." Niels nodded.

Niels and Chuck laughed in unison at their insider joke. Rona pinched herself just to remind her that while acting was a wonderful craft, it could be an ugly business.

"And what do the jumpers get for doing this?" Rona asked.

And once again, their tit-for-tat pitch was resumed. Chuck jumped in first.

"Global broadcast, network coverage, viral media and magazine promotion, residuals…"

"Insurance coverage."

"Whether they succeed or fail."

"And a percentage of revenues."

"And a ticket to the Oscars?" Rona prompted, as a joke.

For a split second, Niels and Chuck took a breath and looked at one another. Niels spoke first and then Chuck responded.

"That possibly could be arranged.

"In addition to which, what is in it for you, is a financial trouble-free future."

Rona was speechless, watching a ball going back and forth across the imaginary net, travelling at an increasing velocity between the two men. Niels served a spin followed quickly by Chuck with a slice. Both of them swopping brief nods of agreement along the way.

"For you…"

"As star of the show there would be…"

"An initial share…"

"Production costs are horrendous these days."

"And on the outside possibility that it may not succeed."

"Which is unlikely…"

"As co-creator of the concept and host of the show, Rona, you would be a constant receiver of marketing perks…"

Rona interjected. "and this will all be contracted?"

"Guaranteed. Once the paperwork is in place. You would be featured as the star of every episode."

"Then after the initial episode was completed."

"…seen by billions of people all over the world."

"Weekly."

Rona held up her hand, took a deep breath and fired a question.

"What would we call this reality show?"

"Ahmmm. The Plungers?", Niels suggested.

"Or? A Part to Die For?"

"That has possibility."

"Oh. Got it. How about 'Do or Die. A Leap for Stardom.?"

"Hmmm. I like it." Niels enthused.

"Stars on a sidewalk."

"Their names on the pavement inside the star."

"What about a beautifully lit plot of fake turf. A small memorial visitor centre?"

"We could sell tee shirts, mugs and souvenirs, that sort of thing."

"Whether they lived to tell the tale or didn't make it."

Rona, to break the momentum, began searching in her purse for her packet of Marlboros and could only ask, "Is this just going to be a onetime pilot?"

"Not at all. We're looking to take it forward as far as it will go."

"A sequel series could follow, 'Do or Die and Dare You Do It Again?"

"Hmm. Might be a little difficult to get enough return guests." That last comment from Niels, slowed the meeting to pause.

"Well, anyway, the point is, we want you up front and centre."

"What do you say?"

"Do you mind if I step out for a cigarette and call Zelda?"

Their pitch was done. They had her convinced and they knew it. Rona took a short break and walked up to the roof of the studio building. She had been working hard to give up her nicotine habit. This was not going to be one of those days. She lit up, took a deep draw and inhaled. Logically, if one was truly committed, why not just jump off of a building like this with only the solid concrete pavement to greet you? Hmm, tomato pie, no way back or out, thought Rona. She began humming "Messy Boulevards." A song on the *The Gormless Experts* album. They were a hot group without question. She recalled reading a piece in an old Hollywood legends book. An English actress named Peg Entwistle had taken a swan dive off the letter "H" on the Hollywood sign in 1932, committing suicide, after the one movie she was in, bombed at the box office. However, these days that would barely register as a news item. It would take the entire assembly of 300,000 extras from *'Gandhi'* leaping one at a time, before anyone noticed. Life in the movies could prove to be a dangerous business. What Rona always recalled, whenever questionable stunts were involved in the making of a project, was the advice of Michael Caine. His book was an inspiration she had read and cherished from her first student acting classes. His paraphrased comments, as she recalled them, conveyed a valuable lesson.

"One of these days, someone on a set is going to ask you to undertake a task that may jeopardize your physical and mental wellbeing. They may tell you, 'I would happily do it myself, but we're running out of time, light and the budget restrictions are such, etc'. Now; I want you to listen very carefully to this, because it is *very* important. You must insist they *show you* how they want it done first, *before you do it.*"

With that in mind Rona decided to accept their offer.

* * *

There was a strong breeze blowing and a forecast of possible rain. Rona stood with one sneaker toe over the edge of the parapet. She found herself staring at the water through the lens of the video camera she had brought along. Reasoning; any footage captured might serve as backup material, should the idea of the series run into problems. The traffic poured in a steady stream across the concrete and steel city bridge. The sound of the metal girders and vehicle wheels engaging gave Rona the same comfort as a giant clock rocking you to sleep with rhythmical repetition. Barges in the harbour stacked with unknown cargo stared back and stayed where they were. Every day across this bridge came streams of people in cars on their way to a job or with a purpose of some kind. Yet not one of them even had the decency to wave or let alone stop to ask what she was doing.

"Surely as I stand here, someone must wonder if I am going to jump. Why wouldn't they stop and ask what I'm doing, perched on the edge of a bridge?" Looking back over her shoulder, Rona pointed her video camera, as the cars disappeared into the web of city streets. Then said into the camera microphone. "Am I looking for someone to save my life or end theirs?"

If this recent, make or break, career move delivered its promise, she would never have to worry about her financial future. Rona knew gambling with your future came with a risk to consider. She wondered;

would she have been smarter to stick with the skills of poker and roulette her parents had taught her? Her mother had worked in a Las Vegas casino and every summer she would see her father return from a tour of second string night clubs across the U.S. He was a good singer all right. He was an even better drinker. And fancied himself as a terrific lover too. Anyway, the truth of the matter was, Rona got to see a hell of a lot of money change hands on the turn of a card or spin of a wheel. Low odds and high cost. Common protocol for anybody working at The Nugget Train was: You commiserate with losers. Give 'em a drink. Losers please owners. Owners reward you. If you thought pyramids in the desert were a treasure, one of those gambling palaces loosened even the tightest leech from the walls of their prosperity. Rona had met a lot of players in those places and made a few. The thing was, after you had made a few, you figured you knew about all of them. And who was to prove it to her otherwise? Maybe one day, Mr. Not Perfect but Mr. Decent Guy, would show up and upgrade her opinion. For the time being she was staying on the acting path. It could be a lot of fun and the chances of winning were about the same.

The water was lapping gently against the girders that held the bridge. What odds would the bookies place on this escapade? Rona calculated it would largely depend on the distance between the leap you made and what was waiting for you when you landed. From this height with water below, you'd be almost guaranteed to surface long enough to change your mind unless rocks were tied to your legs. She felt a chill run through her body. It was getting cold. Maybe it was time to wrap it up for the day. Climbing off the ledge, feeling a little despondent, Rona hoped at least to have enticed a few onlookers on camera and captured interviews for a personal website project, should the proposed series fail to go ahead. About to leave, she saw the figure walking slowly along the bridge path towards her. A woman in her early twenties with a large scarf wrapped around her head, dressed in a billowing coat of orange and green plastic. The woman passed her staring straight ahead. It was then Rona clicked that the coat was actually a parachute. Oh, at last, a real prospect, thought Rona. No question about it. Showtime! The woman stopped ten yards past Rona and dropped the parachute at her feet. She took off her backpack, turned and looked directly into Rona's eyes as though she had known she would be there.

"I saw you on the news. You're the spokesperson for the television series they're promoting. The girl who delivers the last wishes of the jumpers. I assume you do it for a reasonable piece of the action?"

"For a small piece of the action, I am that person," said Rona, accepting the recognition. Are you maybe only looking for an autograph?"

"No, I'm considering being a jumper."

"Oh, a Leapstar?"

"Yes. I wanna know the contract details before I do it."

"Just for talking about it. But not doing it? You 'might' win an audience pass in the survivor show. If you do bravely commit and decide to jump? No comparison. Worth a whole lot more."

"What if a jumper doesn't survive.?"

"Depends on backstory and family history facts. Any noteworthy accomplishments or scandals? That sort of thing. We can negotiate that with your relatives."

"What about dispensation of personal items and costs?"

"We have an excellent broker to ensure your wishes are carried out. A small retainer plus five percent of any cash, jewelry or valuables handled bequeathed to friends and loved ones. Guaranteed delivery."

"You would only take five percent of the cash or jewelry I gave you and promise it would get to the person or people I wanted to receive it?"

"Correct." The woman knew it was a lie and smiled,.

"I wonder if you could get these to that broker."

She held a necklace of perfect pearls in her hand.

"Oooh! Absolutely. No problem. They're beautiful! Are they real?"

"Triple AAA Quality Pink freshwater Akoya pears. Classic and flawless. There's a story that suggests they once belonged to Audrey Hepburn."

"Let me take care of those. We should get on with what you came here to do."

"You mean the jump."

"Yes." Rona held up her RED video camera checking the viewfinder. "Let's do it before the sky changes too drastically. The light is perfect right now."

"Do you want to interview me before I leap?"

"First, let's do a few quick snaps for the front cover of 'Star Bound magazine."

"The front cover?"

"Of course. If we hurry now the light is perfect, this picture is gonna be hard to resist for any newsworthy source."

"What about the video footage?"

"The video would be a lot more effective if you jumped without this," Rona indicated the bulky parachute."

"Oh, and before I do decide, I guess we should be introduced."

"Oh, I'm Rona Cole. And you are?"

"Sara Garret."

They exchanged a handshake and Sara began doing some mediation chants, handling the pearls like they were a rosary. Rona readied the jump contract on a clipboard for Sara to sign.

"So, sign here and we are ready."

"Do I have time to make a call?"

"Are you gonna do it or not?"

"Do what?"

"Jump. Are You Going To JUMP?"

"Hmm, I have to admit I'm having second thoughts."

"You're not sure. Is that why you bought a parachute?"

"It could be," said Sara.

"Would a little help make the difference?"

"How do you mean?"

"Well, you can okay the push box. Right here." Rona indicated a small square on the jump contract.

"A very simple tick would stipulate you've agreed to take full responsibility."

"A push could be helpful. Very helpful. Would it cost more?"

"Approximately a hundred bucks and then we subtract your premium leaper discount. That means you get pushed over the edge for virtually nothing"

"Do I pay you now?"

"We will charge it to your c.c number…"

"Here." Sara Garret unclasping the pearls. "We should put these around your neck, so the water doesn't ruin them."

Rona could hardly believe the exquisite necklace about to be placed around her neck.

"Rona…take good care of them."

"Sara, they will be cherished."

Rona was trembling with anticipation, until Sara appeared to be having difficulty unlocking the clasp of the necklace from her neck.

"Having a problem?"

"It would seem."

"Shall I try?"Rona attempted to take over the removing the necklace, but Sara resisted.

"Easier for me to hold on to them until my very last moment and then put them into your hands."

"You shouldn't make it any harder for yourself than necessary."

"I do have one last request." Sara added, "and a proposition."

"Okay. Let's hear it."

"I am willing to pay you 10,000 dollars if you walk me through this step by step, before I do it."

"You want me to show you first?'

"Yes."

"Have you read the Michael Caine book!?"

"Yes, I have, and I love it. We need to make sure I do this the way you want me to. And ensure its captured in keeping with the project"

"I will guarantee that.'

"That's okay. I brought my own camera crew too," said Sara.

"You bought your own camera crew!?"

"I did. See the men over there on the opposite side of the bridge?"

"Two of them?"

"Yes. They are setting up the shot. And they want you to show them how you prepare someone like myself, taking the jump from the bridge. We can even put a parachute on you. And, on the off chance of an unlikely accident, there is a boat waiting below."

Rona looked over the bridge and now saw a boat in place nearby where jumpers would land. Bouquets of flowers were being scattered by the boat crew. It made for a lovely shot.

"The production qualities are top notch," said Sara soothingly.

"I'm glad you think so, but I'm not the one jumping."

"But you're the one coaching me and…hold on a sec."

Rona noticed Sara signalling to her crew members on the other side of the bridge.

"What are you doing?"

"Just making sure they have a good angle on you."

"Why are they filming me?"

"Chuck and Niels are friends of mine, and they insisted you be included in the initial pilot project."

"I already have a contract with Niels and Chuck."

"Right, they mentioned that, but this is a different project altogether."

"What project is this?

"Together we're compiling a pilot for a new series called *The Stunt People*. Every week we are going to feature people taking a radical chance with their lives. Gamblers like yourself. Extreme adventurers. People who inspire other people to put some pep and zest into the humdrum existence of daily survival."

Sara had managed to unclasp the necklace and began fondling the pearls before handing them over. Rona hesitated, then considered the priceless pearls offered in Sara's outstretched hand. Before taking them, she told Sara, "I will do it wearing the parachute, and only if I get to keep the pearls and get top billing on the show"

"It's a deal. Here let me help you on with this..."

Sara begin to assist Rona with hitching the parachute in place.

"By the way, you should also sign The Push Contract…"

"Right. Okay…"

Rona signed the push box with a big tick. She was firmly clipped into the parachute harness and then signed her name on the contract.

"There we are."

She climbed onto the ledge of the bridge. The parachute inflating behind her. Sara waved to her camera crew. A voice yelled.

"Take One. Series pilot. Stunt or Suicide? Subject One. Rona Cole."

The crack of a clapboard and a split second later Rona felt a gentle push.

"What about the pearls. The beautiful pearls you promised me.....?"

Reaching out for the necklace dangled in front of her, Rona snatched the necklace from Sara's hand. Grasping the string as it broke, she watched the pearls tumble loose and scatter dropping out of sight. The weight of the parachute coiled around her neck. She turned and twisted in the cords and looking below saw only darkness. There was no boat. No crew to rescue her. And no hope. She had gambled her last dream. Images flashed before her as she plunged towards her name etched in cement on the city pavement. SMACK! And then, BOING! She bounced like a feather finding herself floating upwards high above the city, the bridge, the traffic and the people. Hanging out among the stars in the heavens.

"BRRRIINNGGG! BRRRIINNGG!"

Rona woke up with a start. The phone. She picked it up, still half asleep. It was Zelda.

"Rona honey. Were you sleeping? You sound groggy. Had a late night. Are you sitting down? We have some good news. The money Chuck and Niels were looking for. They got it. Confirmed. It's a go. You got the part."

"I got the part!?"

"Yes, Niels wants you in St. Petersburg for May 10th. The contracts are coming to my office and you will need to sign them."

"I don't have to jump?"

"You don't have to what…!?"

"Jump off a bridge…or an office tower or…deal with sharks…I lost my pearls."

"Darling, go back to sleep and call me when you make more sense."

Rona took a few moments to collect her thoughts What an incredible dream that was. She pulled the covers over herself and snuggled back into the pillows. She had learned a good lesson. There would never be a role worth endangering your life for. That was excellent advice Michael Caine gave actors in his book. Rona promised to write it down and tape it to her fridge, "God Bless Michael Caine," she murmured, before falling back to sleep.

(5)
DANCING WITH SCHADENFREUDE

Zoe had just stormed out of the coffee shop. Another argument over adopting a dog. Why was life an ongoing series of issues involving disputes that had simple solutions? Mario wanted to acquire a rescue dog and Zoe did not. He had tried to be reasonable about the matter. Suggesting at least half a dozen different breeds and sizes. From pugs to poodles. To no avail. Zoe wasn't into buying, adopting or rescuing. Her coffee shop exit was the final statement on the subject. Or, that is what she told Mario before leaving him sitting alone holding the tab for her latte and chili glazed doughnut. They were supposed to be on a movie date, having arranged to go to the Coronet cinema for an encore presentation of an old movie. Followed by a special event look-like-a-movie-star contest.

The real irony of it all was that Mario only agreed to go because Zoe loved the glamour of old movies. Also, someone at some time had mentioned in passing, that Zoe reminded them of Sandra Dee. In the movie they were going to be seeing, Sandra Dee was cast as Lana Turner's daughter. So that clinched it. And, Mario believed making Zoe happy would take him one step closer to owning a dog. To hell with it, Mario decided. He would go anyway. Hoping, Zoe would show at the last minute and they would embrace, exchange their apologies and go home together. And that would make it a happy ending. He paid the coffee shop bill and headed for the Coronet.

* * *

Pulling into the parking lot behind the cinema, Mario was still brooding over the disagreement with Zoe. He spotted a small older man heading toward the back of the building. The stooped figure carried with him a black rectangular case and…wait a minute, was that a small dog on a short leash? Mario jumped out of his car and hurried to where the man, about to enter the back doors was fumbling for his keys. Okay, so he must work at the cinema, thought Mario.

"Hey excuse me, sir. Excuse me."

The old man turned around startled. Mario could tell the guy was not in the best of shape. The little brown Labrador puppy was not a happy camper either.

"What. What do you want with me?"

"Do you work here?"

"What if I do?"

"I was just admiring your beautiful puppy.'

"He's a bloody nuisance is what he is, and I don't have time for this right now."

The puppy, meanwhile, was responding to the warm tone and friendly pat from Mario and gratefully licking his hand. Suddenly, the old man without any warning, lapsed into a coughing fit, almost doubling over.

"Not to be rude, sir. Are you feeling, okay?"

"Young man, I'm late for work. And, as they say, the show must go on."

With that, the old guy and the puppy disappeared behind the doors into the back of the building leaving Mario standing alone. If only Zoe could see a puppy like that one, I bet she wouldn't be able to say no, thought Mario. Then he walked from the parking lot at the back to the front entrance of the cinema on the main street.

* * *

The lineup was waiting for the ticket kiosk to open. It was a tearjerker festival week. A selection of movies sponsored by Tearsoft tissues. And tonight, for one night only, the feature was *Imitation of Life,* starring Lana Turner and Sandra Dee. Having recently been voted fifth, as one of the great sob flicks of all time, on the list topped by Bambi. The new improved technical sound and digital print of the film was to be followed by a live Lana Turner lookalike contest and a possible screen test for the winner. Which is why Mario was there. He didn't care if he never saw the movie ever again. As far as he was concerned, he had already seen that movie more than enough. Having grown up with the memory of his mother, after watching this film, weeping into whatever handkerchief or piece of cloth was close at hand.

Outside the cinema, a light rain was falling and the patrons waiting in line were murmuring complaint. The little old lady in the blue bonnet standing behind Mario suddenly spoke up.

"Do you remember ever owning a VCR young man?"

"Oh indeed. The first day it arrived in our house changed my life forever."

Mario found out the old lady asking him questions was named Elsie. And they began a conversation recalling the era before computers with streaming services arrived on the scene. After radio, then television, the average family acquired a VHS player to keep them entertained which allowed them to rent and watch movies of their choice. Once it had been plugged in, other pastimes became redundant. For kids, that meant the dinky toys got abandoned and the Meccano set rusted, left in the yard. Movies were it. Easy access rental, insert video tape and press play. Pause, rewind and eject at your fingertips. Laptops, phones and the internet followed soon after and became the revolution that really influenced and changed everything for everybody. Recalling times of living in a simpler world. Elsie chimed in, interrupting his thoughts with a provocative question.

"Have you seen this movie before, young man?"

"I most certainly have."

"Did you know, in real life, Cheryl, Lana Turner's daughter, stabbed her mother's lover. Killed him. And got off with it.?"

"Oh, I vaguely remember hearing that," said Mario. "But it didn't stop me from falling in love with Sandra Dee."

"Be careful, young man, women like that are dangerous."

"Really? Sandra Dee dangerous?"

"No. Lana Turner. She got married eight times to seven different men and not one of those marriages lasted longer than four years. Which must have inspired the quote she is claimed to have made."

"Which quote was that?"

"She said, her goal was to have one husband and seven children, but it turned out to be the other way around."

"What do you attribute that to?"

"Blonde hair."

"You're kidding me."

"I know it for a fact. I had blonde hair once, and it created all sorts of problems."

"But didn't you also have more fun?"

"The fun I've forgotten. The problems I still have."

Mario had no desire to follow this line of conversation whatsoever. He had one purpose and one purpose only. He was counting on Zoe, his Sandra Dee, showing up before too long. But he had to admit, having a mother like Lana Turner in real life, could prove to be a big problem. Mario commented to Elsie, "My mother watched some movies over and over. Often on a loop. And *The Imitation of Life* was a particular favourite."

"Oh, I do that too. Terms of Endearment and Forrest Gump." Elsie, replied.

"Terms of Endearment I've yet to see."

"Heart wrenching. Keep a three-pack handy."

"I will keep that in mind."

Mario, caught himself looking back. After dinner. His mother glued to the television. *The Imitation of Life* in the VCR. Was there one single occasion when she wasn't helplessly crying by the end of the movie? After witnessing this more than a dozen times, Mario was prepared and readied himself for what he knew was coming. In the movie's story, Lora, played by Lana Turner, a single white mother who dreams of being on Broadway, has a chance encounter with Annie Johnson, a black widow. Annie becomes the caretaker of Lora's daughter, Suzie (Sandra Dee), while Lora pursues her stage career. When Annie dies, the whole soggy saga is resolved when Annie's daughter, having denied her black heritage, throws herself over her mother's casket heaving buckets of tears of remorse and regret. It was a guaranteed Tearsoft sales booster. Leaving those that had watched it, feeling relieved and somewhat smug about their comparatively humdrum existence. So, what was it that made people gain satisfaction from others' misfortune? Did the characters suffering on screen help improve the lives of the audience? Whatever and however it was explained, schadenfreude, when you got down to it, allowed others to temporarily count their blessings. At the expense of someone else. Dancing with schadenfreude was something Mario failed to comprehend.

* * *

Activity in the front of the movie house. Lights switched on in the kiosk to reveal a woman in her early forties, there to do her job but not looking happy about it. Mario stepped forward.

"Two adults."

"One regular, one senior?"

"Two adults."

"You qualify for a senior ticket discount. For your mother?"

The kiosk lady was pointing at Elsie.

"No. Two regular for us," said Mario indicating himself and the vacant space on his right.

"You're waiting for someone?"

"One for me and one for my dog."

"I don't see any dog," said the cashier standing up and looking through the pane of glass with side curtains. "And besides, dogs are not allowed in cinemas."

"Since when?"

"Since 1926…Dogs have never been allowed inside theatres."

"I saw one enter the back door ten minutes ago."

"That is not the same thing at all and you know it. Staff are staff. Patrons are patrons. Dogs are animals."

"Four legged creatures can enjoy watching movies too" Mario challenged.

"Not when I'm selling the tickets."

A patron further down the lineup waiting to get in, coughed politely.

"Excuse me, young man. I am catching a cold just waiting here...would you move it?"

"Well," said Mario to the stubborn cashier. "Could we get our tickets please?"

"You mean for you and her," she said, pointing to Elsie.

"No. I mean us," said Mario pointing to the space on his right. "My dog and I."

"Young man. I don't see a dog, and I wouldn't let it in if I did."

"Is that final?"

"That's final."

Mario looked knee high at the empty, space beside him.

"Okay, Jasper. Home. Off you go," he said.

Mario watched the imaginary Jasper disappear down the street. Every so often he encouraged the dog on his journey by waving his hands. Some of the other patrons waiting in line also followed the invisible dog on its journey. Finally, indicating Jasper was no longer visible and had disappeared from view, Mario sighed in disappointment and then turned abruptly to look straight into the impatient stare of the cashier.

"One ticket" confirmed the cashier, triumphantly.

"Two tickets," said Mario firmly. "Two please."

The cashier almost snarled. "Two," she hissed through her clenched teeth. Taking his money and pushing two tickets under his nose. Mario took one for himself and then pushed the other back to the cashier.

"I want you to hold this second one until a girl named Zoe arrives, this ticket is for her. She will be easy to recognize. The spitting image of Sandra Dee."

The cashier gave up and shushed him towards the theatre entrance. Mario turned around, winked at Elsie and marched through the doors into the movie house. Mario squinted in the dark. Looking for and finding his seats, Row M numbers 6 and 7. He settled down contemplating whether he should buy a packet of Twizzlers or popcorn and a Dr. Pepper. Maybe later. He tried to locate where the lookalike movie star contestants might be sitting. The promos and coming attractions started playing. The audience was settling in. Then the words, "Special Feature Presentation" came up on screen. The chatter of the audience subsided into an odd murmur or two followed by an irritated, "Ssshhhh," among them. The house lights dimmed and the music started. Opening credits began to roll. The words of the schmaltzy theme song sung by Earl Grant echoed in the darkness.

'What is love without the giving / Without love you're only living, an imitation. / An imitation of life.'

You could already hear the first sniffles and the rustle of tissues selected and at the ready. Images of the opening sequence of the movie. Hundreds of people on Coney Island Beach weekend. Among the bikinis, trunks and tans, Lana Turner wearing Cartier sunglasses and dressed to the nines. In a panic. She has lost her daughter and is running around a crowded beach looking for her. Finding her safe, she scoops her up, squeezing Sandra Dee like a rag doll, exclaiming,

"Oh Susie. Oh Susie. Thank goodness. I thought you were lost. I've never been so frightened in my life." Then abruptly, suddenly without warning. KKRUNNKKKK! Darkness! The screen went black and after a minute the lights in the cinema came slowly back on. The unsettled audience began vocalising. Various disgruntled boos and a few yells

"Fix It." "Where's the manager." "Repair the projector!"

Then followed a steady barrage of popcorn and candy wrappers thrown in the direction of the screen. From the back of the house Mario saw an usher come scurrying to the front of the house to make an announcement.

"Ladies and Gentlemen, due to technical difficulties, we regret to tell you tonight's presentation performance and competition has been cancelled and will be rescheduled."

As if in one body, sixteen lookalike Lana Turner contestants rose to their feet in unison to protest.

"What about the contest?

"….the prize money?"

"We have the names and contact information for every one of you and will be in touch with compensation. Once again, management offers their sincere regrets for this unfortunate occurrence."

A stream of loud aggressive comments from the audience ensued.

…"Where is the projectionist?"

…"Are you gonna pay for this sweater. It cost a fortune."

…"Travel costs and one month of my wages!"

…"Mine too."

…"Scam."

…"Rip off."

"…Your popcorn is burnt."

"Where's the butter?

…"Refund the bill for my hairdresser and outfit!"

A chant began building "Money back. Money back. Money back…."

The poor attendant having delivered a thankless explanation fled up the aisle and disappeared.

Standing up, cheered on by most of the audience, sixteen lookalike Lanas, with competition numbers around their necks, left their seats, marching in single file through the exit doors into the foyer, seeking a satisfactory resolution. There was none forthcoming. They stomped out of the cinema and into the evening air. Shortly after, Mario followed their procession and joined them on the street. He saw the blonde heads with their sweater and skirt outfits mingling and chatting. They were extremely unhappy and agitated. He counted the freshly coiffed blonde heads of the lookalike Lanas that were there. Only thirteen? Three missing. Where are numbers two, six, and seven? Then he saw those three get into a taxi and take off.

"Excuse me," he asked Lana Turner number fourteen. "Did you happen to see a girl that looks like Sandra Dee around?"

"Who gives a feck about Sandra Dee! No. I did not."

Lana number fifteen was chatting with number eight and neither of them appeared the least bit interested in talking about Sandra Dee either. They shuffled a little further down the street. Standing on the nearby corner Mario also saw numbers ten and eleven sharing a cigarette.

"Pardon me, Lanas. Did either of you see a girl looking like Sandra Dee."

"There were only two likely Sandra Dees, and they left through a side exit."

"We might need a witness. Did you see what happened in there."

"It's an outrage."

"Someone is gonna pay for this. My boyfriend works for a radio station and …"

Mario did his best to console them. The remaining Lana lookalikes were clustered together. Then the small older man carrying a black case Mario had met earlier, exited the theatre. He led the chocolate brown Labrador puppy on a leash and did his best to sidle down the street unnoticed. Lana Turner number thirteen spotted him.

"That's him. The projectionist."

The lookalike Lanas quickly surrounded him demanding explanation and refunds. Pale and frightened and encircled by angry white blonde hairdos. The man shrunk smaller.

"What's your name?" Lana number five demanded.

"Lou."

"Lou what?"

"Baker. Lou Baker."

The group surrounding Lou was growing. All remaining Lanas joined the melee. Lou, meanwhile, was trying to locate his mobile to phone for help. He found it but Lana number one grabbed the phone and refused to give it back to him. She demanded an explanation for what had happened. To add to the kerfuffle, Yvonne, the kiosk cashier exiting the cinema, joined in. Then a passerby offered to help by calling the police. Mario watched this developing scene unfold from twenty yards away. The dog looked lost. Mario beckoned to the dog. The bewildered puppy headed towards him. The cop arrived. Everyone talking at once. Lana number one was made to return the phone to Lou the projectionist. Lou was doing his best to escape and gasping for air. Yvonne, the cashier, took over as spokesperson, explaining the situation to the cop and pacifying the lookalike Lanas. Glancing in Mario's direction, she turned her attention to him. She said something to the group and pointed to him. It was shaping up like a Buster Keaton comedy. What could Mario possibly tell them? He was not responsible. Nevertheless, he was now the chosen target and a cluster of disenchanted people were heading his way.

Yvonne and the cop with several of the Lanas in the group, marched up to him. Yvonne pointing at Mario, said to the cop, "Officer this is the guy who tried to get his dog into the movie. He was causing a lot of disturbance in the lineup. Agitating other people, who were waiting patiently in the rain."

The cop turned his attention to Mario.

"Okay, young man. What do you have to say for yourself?"

Mario did his best to explain what had happened.

"I planned to see the movie and the contest event with my girlfriend, but we had a disagreement, and I decided to go alone. I tried to buy two tickets on the chance Zoe, my girlfriend, would show up. But this lady misunderstood my good intention."

"So, is this the dog she claims you were trying to smuggle inside the theatre?"

"He wasn't with me, and I wasn't trying to smuggle him in. This lady wasn't having a good day, and I tried to put a smile on her face. Make the difficult job she has to do easier."

The officer looked at Yvonne. Yvonne looked a little sheepish. Mario shrugged a 'forgive me' shrug. Suddenly an urgent call for help erupted from the remaining Lana lookalikes and curious onlookers, clustered around a fallen Lou, lying crumpled on the pavement

"Help. Get an ambulance. This guy is having a heart attack."

All attention was now averted to Lou, turning three shades of red, curled up on the sidewalk groaning. Mario and the puppy headed to where Lou had fallen. The puppy began licking his face. Lou beckoned for Mario to come closer. Mario bent down to hear what Lou whispered.

"Please take care of Cocoa. He has no one to look after him."

Mario nodded. Mario cuddled the dog close to him as the ambulance arrived. The remaining Lanas, Yvonne, the cop and the gaggle of spectators began to move on with their lives. Either doing their job, consoling each other, swopping phone numbers, making coffee plans or calling parents and friends. Mario cradled Cocoa close to him. This was a scene from real life that could have been a movie. The ambulance, having put Lou on a stretcher, took off with the ailing projectionist. And it was at that moment, Mario spotted Zoe waving and running towards him, making her way through the small crowd gathered outside the cinema. Reunited, each with a purpose. Zoe apologising to Mario, who had a question that needed answering and showed Zoe the puppy. Zoe took less than the wag of a dog's tail before she nodded a tearful yes. Then they shared a kiss outside the cinema and everyone applauded. Who doesn't like a happy ending? Glancing first at the departing ambulance, then at Zoe and finally at the grateful puppy they had rescued. Mario, for the very first time, clearly understood what it meant to be, dancing with schadenfreude.

(6)
NOT YOUR AVERAGE JOE

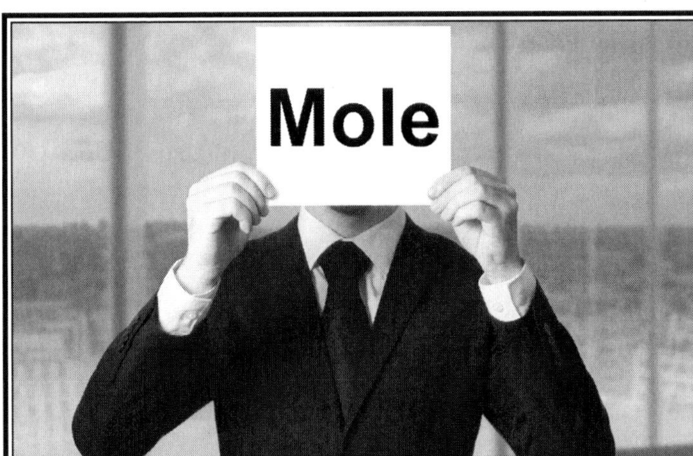

His parents, father Italian, and mother Chinese from Beijing, had three sons, of which he was the youngest. His two brothers were named Romulus and Remus. And he was christened Janus. His twin brothers were both taller, stronger and more handsome, so it was no surprise they got far more attention and recognition than he did. The 'us' at the end of each of their first names being an attempt to bestow a sense of them being a united family. For Janus, that didn't stop what he knew and felt. The gut feeling that he was a somewhat less than important member of the clan. He resolved to do something about that. And spent a lot of his time and energy trying to figure out what that might be. Determined not to be forgotten for who he was. Or, who he might become. And not left out in a garden like a common weed, waiting for someone to mow him down, without due consideration. If anyone was going to do the mowing, he would. At first, Janus tried praying to the various gods and goddesses of his ancestors on both his father's and mother's side for guidance. He included those suggested by his grandparents too. To name a few, Jupiter, Aphrodite, Erh Lang, Apollo, Venus and Kuan Yin. Their exploits and adventures he had read about and were featured characters in movies he had watched. All of them, without exception, were entities of power and influence, still revered and recognized. He wanted to be one of those people. What was it going to take to make him stand out? Janus was okay to look at with an average build. Altogether, he was a perfectly ordinary, well spoken, bright young man. Then; after months of fervent prayers to whomever he thought might be listening, something about his appearance began to change. He wasn't sure which god had made it happen. Or, if any of them had for that matter. But there it was in the mirror, sprouting orange, green and blue strands. The beginning of a rainbow beard. It had curly edges and tiny tufts that emerged on his face that ran tones from yellow to indigo. This, of course, affected his life dramatically. He got all the attention anyone could possibly ask for and more. Mostly inspired by curiosity, astonishment and sometimes ridicule. And not necessarily the kind he was seeking.

"When did that start to grow?" or "Did your mom paint that on you?" and "What's it like having a gay beard?"

Janus told everybody a variation of the same thing, more or less.

"It's been that way since birth. No one knows why it happened to me. It started to sprout orange, green and violet whiskers when I prayed and has grown steadily ever since."

Then one morning he woke up to discover white hairs were replacing some of the coloured ones. Now it was fading. Having a white beard. What would that accomplish? He felt compelled to create a new feature to garner the attention he craved. Or he would be reduced to being virtually ignored once more. And so, Janus Wolf, having grown up speaking Italian, Mandarin Chinese, and English, would set out for the day, catching a bus to take in the local scene in a different community. His favourite pastime became visiting the various malls, coffee shops, restaurants and bars, catering to clientele who were ether Italian or Asian. For instance, when he was in a Chinese restaurant, even though he spoke Mandarin fluently, he would order in Italian. Consequently, chicken chow mein and mushroom chop suey would be ordered in Italian, like this:

"Pollo chow mein e funghi chop suey."

Invariably, this would lead to his finger pointing at the menu and selecting a picture or a number that the waiter clearly understood. Or, conversely when dining at an Italian restaurant if he ordered spaghetti with meatballs, Janus would say,

"意大利面和肉圆."

"Yìdàlì miàn hé ròu yuan."

The fact that he refused to speak English and also chose to speak a language contrary to the native tongue of the establishment he dined at, guaranteed he created a scene around him. The downside was that Janus got kicked out of some excellent restaurants and missed enjoying some wonderful dishes. It also stopped him from ever going back to the same place twice. He'd become known as; the dude with the freaky beard who nobody could understand or wanted to wait on. Speaking only Italian in Chinese restaurants, or conversely, Chinese in Italian restaurants, did provide some enlightening and entertaining moments. For instance, how different cultures with no common language, interact under pressure. However, it soon became clear, that neither the Italians or the Chinese were going to put up with much of that. From then on, Janus did a complete about face. And carried out a total makeover. Shaved off all traces of *any* beard. Wore jeans, a tee shirt, sneakers, a windbreaker with a hoodie. And decided to speak *only* English. Making himself as unnoticeable as possible. He went to all of his favourite restaurants once again. No one took much notice of him. Consequently, people enjoying relaxed conversations in Italian or Chinese and had no idea he knew what they were talking about. And this proved very rewarding. It allowed him to overhear intimate details of private exchanges, without them suspecting he understood. It was like being an undercover spy. Janus loved that. More satisfying than going to the movies because now he could create a fantasy world of his own. Immersed in a shadow life as a secret operative, carrying out imagined dangerous assignments, based on eavesdropped conversations. This newly acquired pastime was inspiring for a while. Janus noticed the most ordinary people you would ever imagine, were often the most interesting. They wanted to get on with their lives and not interfere with yours. Even more surprising, sprinkled among them were genuine heroes, petty crooks, idle dreamers, clandestine lovers, religious freaks, artists, poets and reckless gamblers. Janus took copious notes and decided to find an occupation on a road less travelled. One where risk was required and rewarded. He made up a list of questions to ask himself every day. For instance; How was he going to influence how the world saw him? What would it take for others to sit up and take note of who he was? Without doubt, he accepted destiny was calling, and that it was going to prove an uphill battle to accomplish his ambition. The right opportunity had to be recognized when it showed up. Failure might contrive ways to deter him, but failure was not an option. He came to the conclusion he had no further use for his past memories or current identity. This meant adopting a completely new identity would be necessary. And finding an organization that could put him on the right path. Purely by chance his eye caught a postage stamp size advertisement in *Soldier of Fortune* magazine. The ad promised exactly what he had been looking for.

Make a name for yourself.

A name no one will ever forget.

Freedom from Mundanity!

Intrigue. Travel. Risk and Reward.

Earn yourself a new identity

Grasp your future in your hands!

Fulfill your destiny

Become a winner against all the odds

Adventure and excitement with pay.

Join us today!

Embrace the unquestionable risk you will be taking.

Contact: Recruitment. F.F.O.W. Box 7073 Newark N.J. N.Y. 606491.

Janus filled in the form, mailed it and waited patiently. When the reply came back, it asked for more details. He filled in the information required and then waited a further three months to receive an interview by phone. After that interview took place, he sensed he had aced it and was being considered as a VIP trainee candidate. The official appointment was not given to him at that time, but he was scheduled for a final approval for recruitment meeting and told to be ready to disembark on a yet unnamed mission. Possibly, within twenty-four hours of the final test. A meeting would soon be scheduled with the under-cover officer of the freedom fighter administration department. Code name; Scaramouche.

* * *

The date and time for that meeting had arrived. Today was the day. This was the place. The Take-A-Break Convenience Stop. Washington, D.C. Janus stood nervously waiting inside. The small diner restaurant had a large convenience shopping section. One could buy everything from hand guns to shoelaces. Customers entering were announced by the ding of a bell and when exiting, accompanied by the same. Janus estimated this was almost one year to the day since the first application he wrote. He was impatient and tense, passing his time browsing magazines and considering whether to buy Pringles or Snickers. And then just as he decided on purchasing both, he saw *him*. Scaramouche. Tall, angular and clean shaven. Janus sensed he was an educated man. Who knew how much he knew? He was certainly outstandingly dressed. Wearing a palm beach fedora, a blue silk suit and a white button down, Oxford shirt with a club tie and orange Nikes. Janus thought the orange Nikes were a bit much. Nevertheless, as an undercover agent, it might be imperative depending on the occasion, to be fast on your feet. So, when agent Scaramouche walked into the Take-A-Break for the appointment, there wasn't any doubt about who he was. The woman in her twenties behind the cash register, was texting a friend on her iPhone, and a teenage waitress was cleaning up the small restaurant area. Nobody else was visible in the place. Only the empty tables and a pinball machine in the corner. Janus paid for his snacks and making eye contact, nodded. Scaramouche flipped a bunch of quarters over the counter, took a pack of blue Dentyne from the rack and walked over to the pinball machine. Janus followed, and they nodded before exchanging the bro handshake*. This was followed by a pre-scripted Q and A exchange. It had to be letter perfect, nothing less. The examination was about to begin. Janus had soaked up the preliminary interview questions sent him, like a wet sponge absorbing soap. Now the sweat rolled off his forehead. He felt he was ready. Firing off the first question, Agent Scaramouche expected immediate answers and the completion of the test within seventy-seven seconds. He held a stop watch, pressed it and nodded.

"Got any good answers?"

"I don't give personal information to strangers."

"You don't ask any questions either do you?"

"I ask questions when I talk to friends."

"Have the police ever booked anyone in your family?"

"My cousin Theo for stealing a carton of Camels."

"Where are the walls most likely bugged?"

"In the bedroom."

"How can capture be avoided?"

"Smile for the camera."

"Capsizing cheese heads?"

"Green Bay Packers."

"Name three ships leaving Marseilles in January."

"Rhapsody. The Argentina. The Toucan."

"Radar reading 1714 Lat. 386. What is the place?"

"My apartment."

"What is the opposite of Tranquil Schubert?"

"Rambunctious Shostakovich."

"Complete what's missing when I say Crantz."

"Rosen and Stern Guilden."

"Name the Capitals."

"I'm ready."

"Ecuador?"

"Quito."

"Bermuda?"

"Hamilton."

"Canada?"

"Ottawa."

"Istanbul or Constantinople?"

"Istanbul"

"What about Turkey"

"Ankara."

"Indonesia?"

"Jakarta."

"What about Africa?"

"Which one of the twenty-seven countries."

"Comoros?"

"Moroni."

"Final two questions. How many tablets are in a Mah-Jong game?"

"One hundred and forty four."

"Favourite album?"

""Radio Ethiopia, Patti Smith"

CLICK. Scaramouche pressed the stop watch 72.5 seconds.

"Congratulations."

Janus embraced triumph with almost five seconds to spare. The password exchange verification had been executed perfectly. He'd nailed it. Just then the young woman cashier looked up brightly and said,

"Great poet. Awesome album." Scaramouche picking up on her comment and to avert any suspicion, added,

"So is 'Tuna Laguna' by the Plugs."

"Were you at their concert last weekend?"

"Missed it."

"Oh, too bad. The guitarist is something else. He rocked and then rolled me."

"You know who I did catch recently? The Alligator Ants."

"Oh, the double AA's, great group."

"*Most* excellent band."

"The singer is INCREDDDIIIBBLLLE! Did you know that The Space Twats are from around here?"

The cashier of the Take-A-Break Convenience Stop, was now in complete harmony and joined their conversation, having no idea they were about to verify the next stage of Janus's assignment. Mistakenly, feeling very much included, she rattled on with tips suggesting where uber hipsters, could have a good time.

"So, dope this. The Caribbean last year, The Twats came to the Island where I was staying, and this girlfriend of mine knew this guy who had once played the didgeridoo with Bowie in Australia. He and The Twats used to hang out together and then all this fame happened, and their manager took off with every penny and left them stranded. A case of brass robbery in broad daylight! We stayed with them at the hotel on the beach. Love Island, man. Incredible bonk-fest. In the car park, the dunes, in the swimming pool, even the restaurant. Nowhere was out of bounds. Everything permitted."

Janus recognized drug influenced conversation when he heard it. He no longer had time for the trivial pursuit of where it was heading. Besides he didn't believe anybody made out that much. He never had. Out of nowhere, a guy looking somewhat like a manager approached them.

"Can I get you gentlemen anything from the menu. Coffee?"

Janus and Scaramouche stared back at him and said nothing. So, he left. The cashier now satisfied that there was nothing further worth being hip about, announced she was on a break and disappeared into the back room. Janus looked at Scaramouche knowing their conversation was over. The charged particles previously in the air, were gone. Janus had passed the test, been accepted. And he was ready.

"Well," said Janus. "A pleasure meeting you."

Agent Scaramouche nodded and handed Janus a small brown envelope

"We celebrate your commitment to the cause and bon voyage, Joe Void."

Acknowledging Janus with his new name and identity for the first time, Scaramouche added, "Enjoy your precious freedom and the unbelievable adventure you're undertaking."

"Yes, sir,"

Janus, gave the secret salute of a newly appointed spy mole. Scaramouche returned the salute and then walked to the exit door. Janus felt the loss of imminent departure and asked; "When will we meet again?"

"Future contact for the time being will be arranged by a dead drop. After that, I suggest you attend to events as they unfold."

"Where are you going now?" asked Janus, only half expecting a reply

"I'm off to check out the ghosts in the White House."

"They have ghosts?"

"Indeed, they do."

"And that can be verified?"

"Here's a story for you., Winston Churchill was staying there on a short visit during World War II. One day, he got out of the tub naked and walking into the master bedroom saw Abraham Lincoln, standing by the fireplace. They had a brief conversation before Lincoln vanished."

"Wow! That must have been a bit of a shock!"

"I'm sure it was. For both of them."

"Awesome," said Joe Void, as he saluted again.

"Oh. And I would strongly recommend going to the Ying Yang Dim Sum across the road for happy hour. Have a lychee and rose martini or two. They're delicious. And Joe, be prepared and expect to be named as a person of interest and pursued for a crime you have never committed and presently have no knowledge of. A crime, in fact, that I'm about to execute. That will secure your enrolment as one of us. And, whatever they might try to arrest you for, being entirely innocent as you are, this is America. Remember that. What can they possibly do to you? Good luck with your assignment."

Janus was not prepared to handle this vague parting directive. He stammered, "Are there any final instructions that might be helpful?"

Scaramouche hesitated, then ensuring no one could possibly hear, he moved up close and putting the back of his hand to cover his mouth, he whispered to Janus…

"KMAG YOYO."

And with that, agent Scaramouche walked into the warm evening sun and left Janus Wolf, alias Joe Void, pondering those words.

"KMAG YOYO.?"**.

Obviously, a code name of some kind. A profound secret password? Possibly a covert masonic symbol? At the very least, a record of its historic meaning, will be safely stored and secure in an underground guarded vault somewhere. Janus made a note to track that down later. Most immediate attention was required to attend to his responsibilities as a new mole. Opening the brown envelope, he removed his new i.d passport with an air ticket and a gift certificate enclosed. Wow! This is a one way first class flight to Cairo, Egypt. The gift certificate was a complimentary dinner with drinks at the Ying Yang Dim Sum across the road. Janus decided he was going to head over there right now and just for old time's sake, order Chinese food, speaking Italian. Peking Roast Duck and Moo Goo Gai Pan and whatever else took his fancy.

At that moment, he had no idea, soon, the whole world was going to know who he was. Along with details of an explosive crime, under the headline, 'Foreign Diplomat: Murdered in the White House, Man Wanted for Questioning.' The photo of Janus, with details of the murder, would be featured on the front page of every newspaper the very next morning. And also, broadcast on every media channel, in every language spoken on the planet. With or without the beard, Janus Wolf, alias Joe Void, would now and forever, be infamous.

Footnotes:

**The Bro handshake is a covert series of subtle rapid hand movements used only among undercover agents, spies and moles. .The description of the exchange cannot be revealed here. Anyone caught in the act and participation, faces arrest and interrogation. It is a criminal offence, punishable in 39 states plus ALL of Canada.*

*** KMAG YOYO is an abbreviation for 'Kiss My Ass Goodbye. You're On Your Own'.*

(7)
PRELUDE TO REHAB

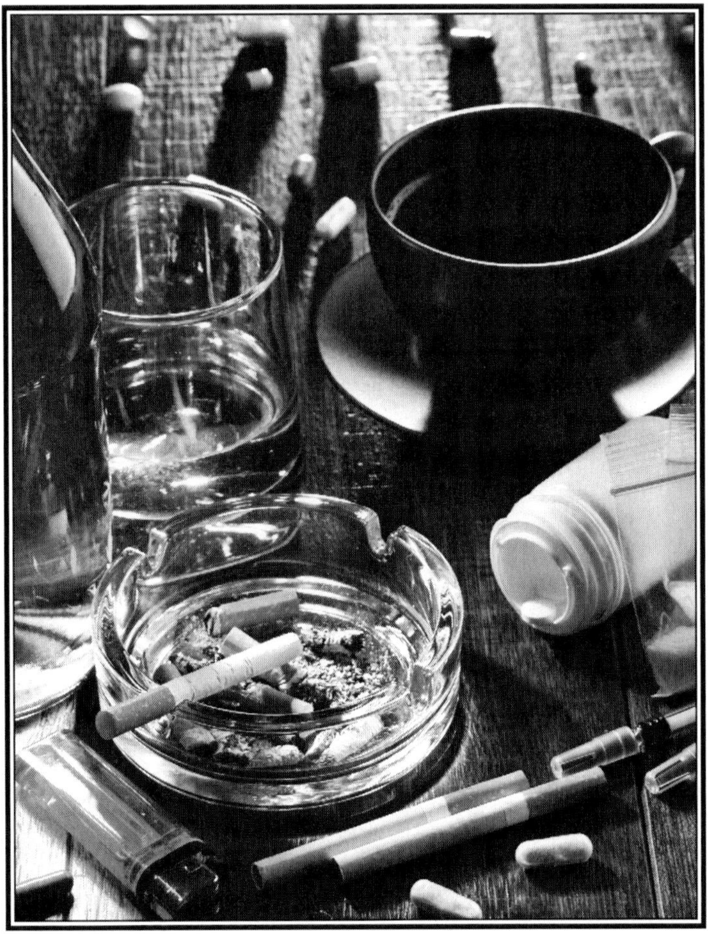

There were several bad habits Veronika was determined to change for the better. That much she knew. Where to start was the problem. You name it, she had promised herself to kick it. But which crutch was going to go first? She lit her second king size menthol filter to go with her third cup of coffee and riffled idly through the magazine, glancing at each page, but reading none. Checking the time, she realized she was late for work. "Shite!." And that is yet another one to add to the list. Being constantly late. There really was no excuse. She had started the day with plenty of time to do what needed to be done. She stubbed out the cigarette.

"My last one," she said to herself.

"You're kidding me," said her next craving, lurking in the shadows.

Her good intentions were playing seesaw bouncing up and down, back and forth, between indulge and deny. The only indisputable fact she had discovered was that god and evil reversed in the mirror of her mind gave her a live dog that had to be fed regularly. Coffee, candy, cigarettes, a joint, a little cocaine on her birthday, uppers or downers. And oh yes, she must not forget to take her valium. This was shaping up to be a stressful day. She was at that time of life that called for using any available excuse. Which is to say, whatever got her through it, one way or another. Almost every evening while enjoying a bottle of wine or a martini or two, Veronika would consider her options. Those options were about to file for bankruptcy. Veronica needed to make a serious commitment. "Tomorrow," she decided, "was it." She was going cold turkey. It would be the first step in preparation for her stay at the Blue Swallow Lodge. These habits she enjoyed were going to topple like skittles, hit head on by a bowling ball. Grappling with them had gone on long enough. Once she had them wrestled to the ground there would be no escape. Forget tap, nap or snap! No options remained. They were done and gone.

Veronika grabbed her coat and purse and headed for the door and then remembered the letter. The letter of confirmation she needed to mail for her reservation at the rehab lodge. That would be the ideal get-away to do some meditation on the issues she needed to face. Already stamped and addressed, she picked up the envelope, clutched it in her hand and headed for her car. Reminding herself at some point, she was going to call Raymond and break off their relationship. He was a nuisance and an enabler. Lots of big talk and a less than average shag. What made her date this guy four inches shorter than she was? That was a no brainer. Answer? Party favours! Now where did she put her car keys? And Yep. She was going to be late again.

She settled back in the car seat and told herself not to panic, she would get there when she got there. She placed the letter for mailing on the dashboard and headed out of the driveway. At least the roads were quiet, and she would have time to peace out with some Michael Buble. Switching her music on, she cruised easy on the usual route to her job at the Home Centre Warehouse. It was inventory time, so the day that faced her was going to be mind numbing. She switched from Buble to Rihanna and tuned to "Bitch Betta Have My Money'. Maybe she could grab a toke or two at the coffee break. That would help. Whoa! Cancel that thought. Her resolution to change a bad habit for a positive one, was already wavering. Okay, a positive step would be to call Raymond and tell him 'adios'. This was as good a time as any. She switched tracks again. This time Drake replaced Rihanna with "Cellphone Bling'. She turned left pulled out her cell phone and hit Raymond's number on her speed dial. His phone rang several times and went to message. Veronika decided to deal with it during her lunch break. She would be a lot more relaxed after popping a valium and smoking a couple of cigarettes. Drake got switched for Bruno Mars taking a 'Grenade.' It took a verse or two with Veronika singing along to those lyrics, before the penny dropped.

"Hold it! Not good thinking. Time out. I need to give myself a good talking to."

She reached for the envelope to the Blue Swallow Lodge on the dashboard. Gave it a gentle kiss. Reminding her what had to be done. The envelope had to be mailed immediately. She pulled up suddenly, changing direction, to head to the post office. When SMACK! Out of the blue. The song changed itself from Bruno to Metallica, banging and bellowing, 'Hard Wired To Self -Destruct.' Any further thoughts Veronika might have had in her head, were obliterated.

* * *

When Veronika came to she was clutching the envelope that *still* needed mailing., she yelled into the empty darkness.

"Is this the Blue Swallow Lodge. Who is in charge here?".

Looking around, she found herself in the middle of a graveyard sitting among a pile of empty booze bottles, pill vials, drug paraphernalia, cigarette cartons, wrappers of endless candy and assorted chocolate bars. Beyond this litter, was a marijuana field with a bright yellow moon overhead. And silence. Dead silence.

"Hello. YoHoo." She yelled.

No one answered or spoke. Veronika was alone in this wilderness. Then faintly in the distance she heard an army of voices marching in unison. They were heading her way. Veronika tensed. She recognized that empty feeling inside. Prepare to do battle. But she would need a line or two first.

"Surprise!" A strange little figure came bouncing out of the cornfield like a jack-in-the-box beckoning to her. "What can I fix for you poppet?"

"Cut the 'poppet' crap and get me out of here tout suit," hissed Veronika. "I have an appointment at the Blue Swallow Lodge and I'm late!"

Pleasantly offering her his outstretched hand, the tiny figure murmured,

"No need for hostility sweet pea. My name is Belmondo. Let me be your candy man. How do you do?".

Veronika checked him out. He bore a resemblance to Raymond but was even shorter. Yes, almost a foot shorter and with a pencil moustache. And wearing a jester hat with silver bells. Violently grabbing his arm, Veronika pulled him down onto the ground and sat on him.

"Where is the nearest post office?" she demanded.

"Post office?" gasped Belmondo, struggling to breathe.

"Yes, POST OFFICE you dumb elf!" she roared blasting several bells off his cap. "I have a very important mission. The name of which must be kept secret. A matter of life and death," said Veronika mysteriously. "Who told you my real name?"

"Your name. What is it. I have no idea?" said Belmondo.

"Hah! I knew it. Withholding information. You are a spy," said Veronika.

"No, ma'am," objected Belmondo. "I am a servant of all people in harmony with satisfying their deepest desires. Believing all beings must be in accord with satiating their appetite to the fullest."

"Oh, shut your door," said Veronika dismissing his ingratiating tone. "Your mouth is creating a draught. Let me warn you. If I catch you messing with my *raison d'être* you're gonna be one very sad fairy. Now, I have a task for you. Here, post this." Veronika stuffed the envelope addressed to the Blue Swallow Lodge between his teeth. "And make it pronto."

"I'm not your delivery boy," Belmondo protested, with his mouth full.

"Then who do you think you are," said Veronika sarcastically.

"I am," said Belmondo, rising to his full four feet seven inches. "The proud proprietor of 'Ta-Ra Presto!"

He spun Veronika around and parted the branches of the giant marijuana plants. Veronika peered through the evening light. There in the small clearing stood a trailer with a silver foil roof sporting vibrant neon letters blinking in the moonlight. 'The Candy Store Café. Always open. Eight Thousand Seven Hundred and Sixty Hours a year'.

"Well, that's quite the welcome sign. I am impressed," said Veronika benevolently. "And as it happens, I am famished. Here, let me help you."

She pulled Belmondo to his feet, yanked the envelope from between his teeth and rammed his dentures back where they belonged. Then smiling sweetly for the first time, asked.

"Now, what did you say your name was again?"

"Belmondo," he said brimming with pride.

"Well Pixie," said Veronika. "After you've served me some party treats, order me a limousine, this letter must be hand delivered."

"My name is Belmondo," he pouted. "And I am not a PPIIXXIIIEEE."

"Excuse me," said Veronika spitefully. "You look like a pixie to me."

"I do, do I," said Belmondo daringly. "Would you like to see it?"

Veronika laughed. "Are you kidding?" she taunted, "You can't afford the exposure."

"Oh no," said Belmondo, meeting the challenge. "Then how about a roll in the fauna?"

"Eat newts you Titch. I would rather die first. But make me a cocktail and we can talk."

And so, half an hour later they were humping in the back seat of the small Volkswagon hitched to the Candy Store Café. And even allowing for the fact, Veronika was sipping on a delicious three olive martini during their coitus, she felt something additional was required for complete satisfaction. First, she needed to get his attention.

"Belmondo, Belmondo, BELMONDO!"

"Eh, what is it, *ma petite cherie*," said Belmondo, stopping abruptly.

"I would like a sandwich," said Veronika unexpectedly.

"A sandwich?" said the puzzled Belmondo.

Belmondo had been hoping she might be requesting a new position they hadn't yet tried. But that was not so.

"Yes, a sandwich you stupid imp. Do we have a problem? This is a café, is it not?"

"Ahhmm. You're right, it is. What kind would you like?" stuttered Belmondo, trying to cope with his required change of focus.

"A simple and reasonable request. An organic, free range Denver, topped with Beluga caviar from the Black Sea," sighed Veronika.

"I'm sorry, we have bread but unfortunately are all out of eggs until Wednesday."

"What! Out of *EGGS!* Do you expect me to settle for a hunk of dry loaf and a lame shag! Have I ridden across the ocean of time into this schizophrenic nightmare for that?" Disengaging his diminutive frame, Veronika roared vehemently in his face.

"You little creep. I demand a full refund."

"But you haven't given me a dime." gasped Belmondo. "How about an ice cream to cool you down, instead?"

Veronika was about destroy him forever when her muse intervened with a change of mind. A moment of untypical benevolence swept over her. She enquired prettily.

"Hhhhmm. The right flavour might earn you a reprieve. What do you have?"

Belmondo, in a quicksilver response, in what he hoped would grant him a reprieve, concocted a preposterous menu of possible life savers. "Pineapple Pumpkin Seed, Alfalfa Fizz, Cherry Galore, Catalino Pear, Okalla Banana, Chamomile Cornets, Spanish Gin, Grand Canyon Chomp, Elderberry Buds, Locust Bean dunked in Maple Syrup, Coca Mocha, Poppy Parfait, Jelly Baby Razzle Dazzle and …and.. Vanilla with a Malt Vinegar topping." spluttered Belmondo,

"HHhhhaaahhh," Let me think about that for a moment," Veronika pondered.

Belmondo prayed her choice would be the right one. Veronika shifted her weight thoughtfully, allowing Belmondo to regain some of his lost aplomb before she replied.

"The cherry is tempting...but give me the vanilla and malt vinegar."

Belmondo breathed a sigh of relief and pulling himself out of her danger zone, skipped across to the ice cream machine and pressed vanilla. PPLLOOPP!! The measured helping of thick vanilla ice cream, fell into the waiting cone and Belmondo topped it with a hearty helping of extra thick slurpy malt vinegar.

"Here we are. Made just the way you like it."

Belmondo handed Veronika the cone, which she consumed in two gulps.

"Yummmeee, delicious" moaned Veronika after inhaling the cone. "Now...what about my sandwich?"

"Ehhmm, Right. Sandwich. I've got a better idea. Let's go out to eat instead. The night is purring soft and warm. We can dance the hoochie coochie until daybreak illuminates the tapestry of tomorrow."

"You know," said Veronika in a quiet afterthought of compassion. "You have a certain élan. Somewhat hard to resist but, then again, impossible to take seriously. So, let me be very clear with you, about this. I do not want to go out to eat. *MAKE ME A SANDWICH!!"*

The blast of her venom, ripped the gingham curtains of The Candy Store Café from their rods. And so it followed, later that evening, Veronika, brimming with frustration, watched Belmondo opening a can of spam, spreading discarded bacon fat on stale bread, while whistling *What A Wonderful World.* No tune annoyed Veronika more than that one. She was bubbling feverishly and about to burst.

"My cure or my money back. Where is the limousine to take me to the lodge?" Attempting to soothe her, Belmondo began doing his best Smokey Robinson imitation.

"Baby, Baby," crooned Belmondo. "Why resist what we have going on?"

"Bug off, you pest," scathed Veronika with emphasis.

"Baby, baby," smoothed Belmondo. "Cool the lava and meditate on the principle of clear profit that we are going to generate. Translated that means, more success together than apart. A business plan."

"What kind of business, exactly?" Veronika replied, drumming her razor sharp red fingernails on the formica café table

"We can offer customers a ride in your pleasure capsule until daybreak. Once the word gets around, they will line up around the block. We will have a pack of hungry dogs hooked for a comeback. Now, I do believe that makes a great future for us as a team. We know how to have a good time together, *n'est-ce pas*? I am all you will need along with my endless supply of treats."

To make his point, Belmondo, was busy filling a spoon and lighting a match underneath the contents.

"Here we are, honey bunny, a loving spoonful. And plenty more where that came from."

Veronika rolled down the window of The Mobile Candy Store Café and took a deep breath of the aromatic marijuana plants wafting in the air. She had no intention of being pimped out by a bossy pixie. Meanwhile, Belmondo unaware he was treading on a bubbling volcano, continued yak -yakking his business proposal.

"Besides, we need each other like flowers need the rain. *Comprendez?*"

That was it. Veronika could no longer contain herself. Grabbing Belmondo by the throat, she erupted in full splendor ripping a hole in the roof of The Candy Store Café. And as if he were no more than the cap off a cola bottle, she hurled Belmondo into the great beyond. "AAAARRRGGHH. GET ME TO REHABBB." she screamed. Her cry for help echoing unanswered. Veronika felt herself spinning out of control before losing her breath and collapsing. She was spent. Looking up through the jagged edges of the silver foil rooftop, she stared into the sea of endless space. She had nothing left. There were no stars. Just darkness and this one last desperate thought: "Now I know what it feels like to be the last cornflake in the packet." She found herself, once again, stranded in the wilderness. Alone. With only the familiar rumbling of an endless storm, howling and whistling, carrying the name of the deadliest addiction of them all.

"SHUUgaaaRRrr. SuUgGaarRRRR. SuUUGGARrrR. SUUggaarr. SugGGar..Sugar!!." "Hola!. Help. Is anybody out there?" Silence. Veronika slumped in despair."Even those bastards at the Blue Swallow Lodge have abandoned me!" And then blackout.

* * *

"How are you feeling, miss?"

"Where am I?"

"You're in the hospital after your accident."

"What happened."

"You were lucky."

"This is what lucky feels like?"

"Your parents and friends have been calling to see how you are. Anything I can get you?"

"I would kill for a cup of coffee and a cigarette."

"We're looking to discharge you tomorrow. So, you will have to wait a little while longer. Dr. Kendall strongly recommends you taking it easy for a couple of weeks."

* * *

Two days later, Veronika was back in her kitchen. After pouring the steaming hot coffee into a large mug, she scooped three heaping spoons of refined white sugar, stirred them into the liquid and licked the remaining granules off the spoon. Reaching for the pack of menthol filter on the kitchen table, she lit one up, took a deep drag and exhaled. "How would I ever get along without a little help from my friends?" she reminisced. She made a promise to herself. "Once I am fully recovered from my car accident, I'm going for the treatment needed to the Blue Swallow Lodge rehab facility." The front door buzzer interrupted her thoughts. 'Breep. Breep. Breep.'

"Oh, that must be Raymond. He said he would drop by with a little treat to pick me up. Such a doll." Veronika headed out of the kitchen to open the front door to let him in.

(8)
THE CHICKEN CHRONICLES, PART ONE: EDWARD

The unidentified voice was blaring.

"We are going to have to invest in the artist to show us the way because there never has been a time when the preservation of this extraordinary planet we live on more needed creative healing. It's in a right mess!"

Nelson Drum walked over to the radio and switched it off. Opening the refrigerator, he peered inside and addressed the cellophane wrapped container.

"What the feck is the world coming to, Edward?"

Nelson was talking to the dead chicken again. There was no knowing how long it had been since Edward was vertical and clucking around a chicken coop. Hopefully, when he was alive he had experienced the warmth of a sunny day or two before he'd met his end. Nelson had purchased Edward yesterday at the local supermarket. And truth be told, it was actually slightly less than half of Edward, that Nelson was talking to. He had thought to ask Edward where his missing parts might be but then decided against doing so. There were other questions Nelson felt needed answering before that. One thing is for certain, nothing much had changed since Edward's death, except maybe Edward's colour. He presently lay, for what could be called his final viewing, uncooked on a plastic tray on the second shelf inside Nelson's Westinghouse fridge. And though Nelson had quietly whispered to Edward, "For better or worse," Edward had definitely got the worst of it. He was undoubtedly deceased. And not only mort but eviscerated. Some of his pieces AWOL and elsewhere. Nelson happened to be talking to Edward's left wing, breast and thigh bone. If he had owned the very latest 'DNA Map Laser Detector' by Geiger Gadgets, he would have detected that Edward's right wing, breast piece and thigh bone, had been picked up from the same supermarket location twenty-four hours earlier by Vladimar Koppel, an immigrant filmmaker from Estonia. Vladimar was a recent arrival to the USA and had managed to shoot a film on the subject of cannibalism in the south of China covering the first decade of the 3rd century B.C. And even though the film had been nominated and received several awards in the Orkney Islands Film Festival, this was America, and they didn't give a crap about what was going on in other countries, unless it made a lot of profit for the U.S. of A. Which was fair enough once you understood their rules. Nevertheless, filmmaking found Vladimar often hungry and without much money. However, he had recently received a belated royalty cheque. And the good times, although rare, were meant to be enjoyed. So, it turned out Edward's right thigh, breast and one wing departed with Vladimar Koppel on their way to his art loft not two blocks away from Edward's other half. One might be tempted, at this juncture, to claim what Vladimar had purchased was, 'the better half'. However, the case for that was pending and uncontested because Vladimar had failed to christen his half of the chicken, with a proper name. And, we can assume Edward was blissfully oblivious to these facts. Therefore, nobody could object and there was nothing to stop Nelson from talking to Edward. The processed carcass sat there speechless. This guaranteed Nelson was uninterrupted while peppering the dead chicken with unanswered questions.

"So, Edward, is there anything I can get you in your final hours?"

"If you could change anything about your appearance, what would that be?"

"Do chickens dream?"

"Are you missing your other half and pieces?"

Edward had no other option but to play dumb. Nelson decided it was time to prepare the evening meal. Before doing so, he reached into the inside door of the refrigerator and took a bottle of sarsaparilla from the rack. Pouring himself a glass he took a swig, hoping it would alleviate a problem he was having with toe fungus. Then, lifting Edward from the plastic tray, Nelson reached into a kitchen cupboard, opened a cardboard box, removed one of the small plastic bags it contained and filled it with the included packet of crumb coating. Dropping Edward into the bag, he began shaking Edward's parts, while improvising the lyrics of an old Frank Sinatra tune.

"So, goodbye my friend we've come to the end of a brief episode. Give me one half of chicken and one more glass of Coke."*

**We should accept as fact, Nelson knew sarsaparilla was closer in appearance and taste to root beer. The reason he likely substituted the word "Coke" was that neither sarsaparilla nor root beer were as easy to rhyme in any song as Coke is. However, to proceed…*

Placing Edward's coated parts on the baking tray, ready for the preheated oven, Nelson said his fond farewell in the empty kitchen.

"As a gift to you on your final moments prior to baking, I raise my glass and salute. To good friends and the end of world hunger. *Skol*!"

He chugged down the rest of the sarsaparilla and thrust the drained glass above his head. Nelson then placed Edward's crumbed left half in the oven, set the timer for forty-five minutes, (because Edward was still bone in), and retired to his living room couch. He switched on the remote and tuned into a streaming film channel. The first hint of future serendipity found Nelson watching the film Vladimar Koppel had directed two years ago. Almost, at that very same moment two blocks away, Edward's somewhat better dressed yet unnamed other half, was being cooked after being doused with olive oil and herbs. Soon to be devoured, Vladimar was contemplating Edward's crispy skin and juicy meat being washed down with a bottle of budget savvy Chilean chardonnay.

N.B.: We felt it worth noting for our readers, to update the whereabouts of Edward's remains. His head, neck, giblet, back and toes, were packaged inside a freighter frozen storage container on its way to a pet food factory in Alaska. To continue….

Vladimar, having placed Edward's cooked right half on a Royal Dolton china plate, picked up at a local thrift store, settled down to read the latest edition of Filmmakers Monthly. The article that caught his eye featured opinions as to why so many awful movies make so much money.

"What a load of bollocks!" Vladimar said to Edward's right leg before sticking it mindlessly in his mouth. "Justifying why success encourages failure to repeat itself. Rubbish is rubbish so why pretend otherwise?"

Vladimar took film making seriously. As a kid, up close and personal, he had studied insects as they traversed upside down and side-ways, crawling out from under rocks, clinging to trees, ceilings, corners of nooks and eaves, observing life on the planet from unusual angles. "That must be so awesome cool," he'd figured. And as soon as he managed to get a camera in his hands, he set out to interpret the world from this skewed perspective. It hadn't made him rich, but always hungry for more. Now he was contemplating what his next movie project might be. Taking another large bite of Edward's right leg, Vladimar threw the magazine carelessly over the back of the couch barely missing the glass seagull he had won at the Orkney Film Festival. He loved the movies. Even if he had nothing to eat, images provided food for his imagination. And that appetite could be indulged whether those images were moving or still. *National Geographic* magazine, for instance, made him believe he was there among the animals and people from distant lands. Exotic faraway places that made him feel warm and alive. Part of the living breathing beating heart of nature. He reached for the next magazine on the unread pile. '*Your Personal Health.*' This edition promised to outline Medical Anomalies. Vladimar, according to their reports, had a congenital condition. This condition familiar and comfortable to him, was now filed and classified after extensive tests and research, as 'Gecko Syndrome.' An oddball prognosis requiring treatment with no guaranteed cure. The simple truth was that, on occasion, he liked to wander after midnight, climb trees in the middle of the city or shuffle upside down in his Neo-Sucker boots adhered to the walls of buildings. Nothing weird intended. He enjoyed doing it. And nobody was harmed. Case closed.

Rejecting the magazine in disgust, he ripped off the rest of Edward's leg and threw the bone at the mini basketball hoop he had set up on the back of the apartment door. The bone missed the hoop basket by a couple of inches. Vladimar figured it would still be there when he went out to empty the garbage later.

"What cheap mindless label makers science has turned us into. Do we have to put an identifying tag on everything?"

But there was no point dwelling on problems in life. He was reminded of a song his mother had sung to him as she bounced him on her knee as a child. A remedy that always worked when he felt a cloud hanging over him. He began humming and singing;

"You gotta accentuate the positive. Eliminate the negative. Latch on to the affirmative. Don't mess with Mister In-Between."

Those words always turned on his creative juices. His inner gecko was demanding to get out. That urge to put on his boots and walk upside down on walls and ceilings. And even though it was way before midnight and way to early to roam the city streets, he had set up a workout program he could do in the loft. He put on his Neo-Sucker boots, bounced into his personal play area, stuck on his virtual reality helmet and pushed the action button on the video wallpaper channel. First, he ran up one wall to the ceiling and back down, then began dancing among the wild animals leaping through the jungle of stock footage emanating from his wall and ceiling. Finally, after breaking into a mild sweat, Vladimar had a moment of profound inspiration. He was going to hitch a ride to nowhere in particular, take his camera with him and collect footage for another movie.

Meanwhile; picking over the salad laying next the cooked bird, Nelson pursued his running heart to heart exchange. About to polish Edward off, he adopted a very subtle approach and continued a gentle tone of questioning.

"Did you suffer psychological problems with the over-crowding you experienced?

Was there enough time to make any friends before you were separated from them?

What was your last thought before they severed your head from your body?

Do you recall seeing the name tag of the person who did it?

Would you recognize them if you ever saw them again?"

To his credit Nelson stopped short of asking Edward why he had crossed the road, realizing that had likely never happened. Finally, having exhausted his search for satisfactory answers, Nelson settled on a resolution. He was going to track down Edward's executioner and assemble a portfolio taking snapshots of people at work who killed chickens every day. An ambitious task indeed. In the United States alone, it's estimated somewhat close to ten billion chickens are killed for their flesh each year. But if that could be accomplished, Nelson might possibly write a book.

And that is how two halves with some missing parts came together. Vladimar found himself thumbing a lift on the outskirts of town when Nelson came along in his VW camper and offered him a ride. It took only a brief exchange for Vladimar to realize

Nelson was on a passionate mission. And a passionate mission was exactly what Vladimar was seeking for his next film. Did either of them guess or even suspect that it was the spirit of Edward that had brought them together as conscientious carnivores? That never crossed their minds. Not for a second. Leaving Seattle, as they headed to Arkansas, Edward was history and there was no way to track how the serendipity of one dead chicken had united them in a common quest.

* * *

Across the other side of the country in a warehouse full of junk, the mechanical butcher that severed Edward's head from his body, lay kaput. Having handled up to a thousand chickens at a time, lined up in uniform rows and then dispatched with a single commiseration. 'Adios.' Now, the mechanical butcher with the rusty blade, suffered ignominy in silence. Abandoned in the darkness after so many years of solid service and hundreds of thousands of severances. The various machine parts working so effectively for so long, dismantled and dumped, in a scrap yard. With no plaque forged in recognition of industrial services rendered.

The various chickens in their pieces or whole, travelled a far different journey and chain of events. From death to cleaning, packing and wrapping. Then came their distribution, promotion, purchase, preparation and cooking. Then, onto plates or into boxes. Roasted, barbecued, carved or coated, cooked in sauces, added to pasta, or, as an ingredient for stews, soups and sandwiches. Each chicken or a part of each, was heading for somebody's mouth. Mouths of all ages, races, shapes and sizes.

Arthur Hobbs, the operator of the mechanical butcher that had ended Edward's life, had long since left his job at The Fortune Meats Company. They were the largest meat preparation and packing conglomerate in the country. In stark contrast and unquestionable irony, Arthur was on record as being the shortest time employee ever. The moment he saw Edward's head leave the body, Arthur tried unsuccessfully running for shelter, to avoid the initiation of a blood stain. Nothing against union rules, that is true, but it proved very unpopular among his employers and fellow co-workers. They understandably felt slighted for being callous chicken killers compared to this conscientious objector on the same payroll. Facts being what they are, everyone has their own conscience to deal with. Arthur Hobbs was a registered trainee employee of Fortune Meats for the grand total of 88 minutes, but he was to leave the company an enlightened man. The two drops of chicken blood that fell on his protective overalls had inspired him to become a vegetarian. Also, for the very first time in his life, he had experienced strong feelings for another living creature. He had shared Edward's final glorious moment. They would always be...well...friends. Let other people call him chicken-shit for quitting. He didn't care. He visualized his friend was in some kind of poultry heaven. From that day onwards, Arthur had the same recurring dream. Thousands of chickens running free in an open meadow with no fences. Though he was often ridiculed for being convinced that his dream was a message from above. That was his prerogative. And his story.

After they located Arthur living in a monastery in South Dakota, his experience was recalled filmed and chronicled by Nelson and Vladimar in preparing the beginning of a much larger project*. Nelson tabulated Q & A sessions with Arthur, while Vladimar recorded extensive footage for his movie project**. Arthur having co-operated with their intrusion, insisted on including the following dedication:

"We are all hopeful that Edward will be clucking happily ever after, having ascended to an after-life someplace, where chickens can enjoy decent food and exercise."

Footnotes:

**'The Complete Chicken Chronicles' will be available from Cascade Print & Audio Books NYC. in 2021. The introduction to Nelson Drum's book, contributed and written by his therapist, states his patient was inspired by visitations from the ghost of a partial chicken looking for his missing parts. Nelson referred fondly to this apparition as 'Dwa'. The obvious connection being 'Dwa' contains three letters that are part of the chicken's full name. And, although he fully believed in the chicken's ability to listen to his questions, his therapist assures us, Nelson always understood, Edward was never quite all there.*

*** Vladimar Koppel was able to obtain funding for editing his latest film, "The Chicken Killers.'*

(9)
THE FUTURE OF PLEASURE

Molly blinked. In between the ducks on the pond and the city skyline, a convoy of cars moving across the distant bridge, sparkled like jewels on a necklace. Tinsel Town, she thought as she watched the shimmering headlights.

"Enjoying a quiet summer evening?" said the stranger sitting on the park bench next to her.

Not wanting to engage in conversation, Molly politely nodded back in the affirmative. She was waiting for Arnold, her boyfriend and looking forward to a quiet dinner together. Hoping there was an event soon be announced that had not been scheduled. Maybe Arnold was going to ask her to marry him. They had been engaged for almost fifteen months, and everyone said they were made for each other. The man beside Molly reached inside the plain brown bag he carried with him and pulled out what appeared to be a Pez dispenser. She had never seen one quite like this. Two devil horns on a lascivious looking Mickey Mouse.

"Does Walt Disney know they're messing with Mickey?" was the thought that crossed her mind.

The man smiled a knowing smile and popped two silver tablets from the Pez dispenser into his mouth. Then he spat them in the direction of the pond. PPPRREEEEEEP, PPPPRRRREEEP. Two ducks disappeared. Did Molly only imagine one of them turned into an orange bat and flew away? The man never moved or commented. He seemed to be content to wait for other potential targets to appear and was in no hurry.

"How awful", thought Molly. "I wish Arnold would get here. This joker could destroy every last one of them ducks if he doesn't arrive soon."

Molly stole a glance at the unassuming man sitting beside her. He didn't look threatening. A brown jacket and pants, soft casual shoes. A baseball cap with a logo. Molly tried to make out what the logo said but sitting beside him made that difficult without standing up and looking down at him.

"Orwellian Pharmaceuticals," the man said pleasantly. "It says Orwellian Pharmaceuticals."

"Oh. That's who you work for? And you have a local office?"

The man smiled popped two more silver capsules in his mouth and spat out the husks. PPRREEEP. PPRREEEP. A sparrow nearby turned into a cartoon seagull and another duck disappeared. A fox appeared out of nowhere and then ran into the nearby bushes.

"I know what you're thinking," said the man. "You're going to contact the authorities and tell them I am destroying the local wildlife."

He held up the brown bag "Before you do that why don't you try one? Any colour but the silver." Molly recoiled. She looked around. Nobody around. Where was Arnold?

"Not for me, thank you. What are they?"

"Moodatoms. We're currently running tests in the market. Milwaukee today. Pittsburgh on Friday. Sydney, Australia next month."

Molly imagined koala bears, kangaroos and parrots vanishing by the dozen. Possibly becoming an endangered species if this guy carried out his tests.

"Moodatoms are like Skittles or M&Ms but a whole lot more fun. And soon they'll be available at your local convenience store, if I have anything to do with it."

The man found this very amusing. Molly was alarmed.

"They look like they should require a licence."

"The company has gone through all that rigmarole. Not required. Orwellian Pharmaceuticals has a lot of friends in the right places."

Molly decided this wacko should be incarcerated or, at the very least in an institution where he could be placed under observation, questioned and treated. She was going to have him arrested for questioning when Arnold got here. Meanwhile, better to humour him and play along.

"These Moodatoms, are they good for you?"

"Mood enhancers. Try one and see."

"No, thank you. Like I said, I'm waiting for my boyfriend. He'll be here soon. He's a police officer."

"Probably delayed by the celebration event going on downtown."

"Celebration?"

"It's just getting warmed up. Sit back and enjoy the firework display."

"Fireworks. Is that what brought you here?"

"I did what I came to do. Time to watch the results."

"What do you do at this company you work for."

"You could say I'm a salesman. Recently appointed national supervisor with a promised promotion ahead to Worldwide Distribution Manager."

"Sounds like a promising future. But couldn't you be selling a product that was less..."

"Moodatoms are not harming anything. Although they might appear to be so."

"It sure does look that way to me."

"I know. We have been trained to deal with the first reaction people have to our product but believe me the average plastic bottle is causing a lot more threat than these. You really should try one."

He offered Molly the bag. Molly looked into the bag he was holding out to her.

"They're different colours."

"Yes, they are. All different. Depending on the mood you want to experience. Avoid the silver capsules. Not for beginners."

"Why?"

"We are only promoting the various coloured Moodatoms for the time being. If you swallow one of these depending on the colour chosen, it will change the world around you and your interaction with it. But, Silveratoms are designed for future use. They will transform the molecules on the object they impact. Watch"

The man from Orwellian Pharmaceuticals placed a silver capsule on the tip of his tongue and aimed it a curious squirrel nearby. POOF! The squirrel disappeared, replaced by a kaleidoscope of colourful butterflies. And then they too were gone. Molly was hesitant but more than curious.

"What do the green ones do."

"Go ask Alice."

"Alice?"

"Like the song says. One pill makes you larger. One pill makes you small. And the ones that mother gives you don't do anything at all."

Molly popped the green capsule in her mouth and swallowed.

* * *

The shiny black squad car of Arnold Costa roamed through the downtown core. There was an unusual tension building in the city. It told Arnold to expect the unexpected. Shaping up to be a 'no holds barred public party till you drop' atmosphere. Whatever this event was that had arrived in the community would require very careful monitoring. The whole downtown core had been transformed. Giant video screens stretched across the main streets were lit up with a message pulsating on the screen.

"Moodatoms. From Orwellian Pharmaceuticals. Coming soon to a city near you."

The promo message accompanied by a soundtrack subliminally chanting. Moodatoms. Moodatoms. Moodatoms. Moodatoms. Moodatoms. The individual letters of the brand name flashed on the screen, dissolved and gradually changed shape. Separating into their various colours and properties. Each one becoming recognizable as a capsule with a distinct and guaranteed mood changing potential. Various filmed social scenes and appropriate music supported each type of Moodatom available and the mood enhancement it promised.

THE BLUES. An easy beautiful warm time to enjoy your shade of blue, whether sky, ocean or cobalt.

THE GREENS. Fresh. Vibrant. Enlivening. A new viewpoint with an eternal horizon.

THE YELLOWS. Rhymes with mellow and indeed it is. No clouds in your coffee with this capsule.

THE REDS. Strong. The pulse of the world at your fingertips. Hot and sexy. Feel the urge. Take the plunge.

THE INDIGO. Purple Brain. Doors will open that allow you to follow the road you choose to explore.

THE TRANSPARENT. Restores your original mundane mood.

THE SILVERATOMS. Look to the future for this exciting development that will transform the world you live in.

Expectations were running rampant. The mass of people gathered cheered in anticipation of a wham-bang weekend. Huge tent booths with Orwellian representatives in attendance had been installed downtown. The various Moodatom colours were displayed all over the city. Information pamphlets were passed out that emphasized that all capsules come in different strengths.

'We recommend the lowest grade to get you rolling. Supplies are limited. A 'no responsibility' contract needs to be signed before samples of your choice are dispensed. You will be aware of several paramedic units ready for action if necessary. Follow the simple guidelines and they will have nothing to do.'

* * *

The man still sitting next to Molly on the park bench, appeared on screen as the spokesperson for the Orwellian Pharmaceuticals Co. His relayed image twenty five feet high was accompanied by deafening cheers from the eager audience.

"Hello, mood explorers. My name is Oliver Black, area sales supervisor for Orwellian Pharmaceuticals. We're here to bring controlled safe, exciting 'mooding' to you, ladies and gentlemen. Young and old. Every race and culture included. We live in difficult times. With demanding jobs and responsibilities. Commitments, that we are expected to fulfill each and every day. People need pleasure. And all of us will seek and find pleasure whether it is granted or not. Orwellian Pharmaceuticals believes pleasure should be part of what we deserve. Enjoyed without question. Enjoyed without fear. To activate that right, we've stepped into the role as a global leader to guide and supply how pleasure is safely administrated. Moodatoms have been researched, tested and have proven themselves within strictly supervised parameters. Your safety is our promise. The present national crisis with opioids is the result of untested and crudely made products. Either the homemade garden shed variety or even less reliable. Those imported from other countries, without registration approval before they are distributed on our streets, in our schools and neighbourhoods. These dangerous compounds are causing hundreds of unnecessary casualties daily in every major city across the world. We at Orwellian Pharmaceuticals have created a solution to enable people to enjoy pleasure with minimal risk. Pleasure moods should be a basic human right, as much as the air we breathe. In the large coloured tents, erected specifically for this occasion, you will be introduced to a series of laboratory tested mood enhancers designed under scientific laboratory guidelines to bring a guaranteed measure of pleasure to your everyday life. Before I turn this remarkable event over to you for your sensual mood enjoyment, let me ask you this. Shouldn't we all be able to enjoy a change of how we experience our day? Rearrange the scenery of the play we take part in, moment to moment, day to day? The play that can be titled "Every Day of Our Life?" In which we are expected to fulfill our role, whether we like that play or not. Surely, each and every one of us, deserve the opportunity to embrace a change we can choose. A change of heart. A change of mind. A change of tactile connection. And, if not, why not? Orwellian Pharmaceuticals introduces Moodatoms, the future of pleasure."

The crowd erupted. They were ready like lemmings to take the leap. Wherever it landed them. They were willing to go. The ceremony opening ribbon was cut. And the party was on.

* * *

Molly was watching the sky above the city building change colour. It shifted and spilled mixing one colour overlapping and intermingling with the next. Green, blue, yellow, and indigo an orange and then dark red turning the skyline into one giant roman candle. A beautiful butterfly sky. The rumbling voices emanating from a mass of bodies filled the evening air.

The man from Orwellian Pharmaceuticals looked at her and smiled. "I think I hear the sound of animals being released from their cages."

"What is happening?" Molly wondered.

Oliver Black leaned back on the park bench and began to sing; "Something tells me it's all happening at The Zoo." Molly recognized the line from an old Simon and Garfunkel song and smiled meekly.

* * *

Downtown indeed, it was all happening. Without warning, a sporty lime green Mercedes came screeching to a halt blocking Arnold's patrol car. A beautiful blonde in a bikini jumped out of her car and into his and stuck an ivory handled derringer into his face.

"Excuse me officer. I can tell you are no ordinary cop. Got a light?" she said huskily. Arnold did not twitch an eyebrow. He was no ordinary cop. And he looked like a movie hero.

"My pleasure," he said flicking his Bic disposable. When the blonde in the bikini noticed she was holding a gun, not a joint, she apologized.

"1 am sorry I thought it was cigarette. How silly of me."

"No problem, Miss," drawled Arnold. "I'm glad to be of assistance." The bikini clad woman put the gun away and offered him the bag she was holding.

"Try one of these instead. Maybe two? Moodatoms in three colours. Such a rush."

"No, thank you, Ma'am, I'm on patrol." The busy traffic was piling up all around them. The blonde stranger jumped out of Arnold's car and back into her Mercedes, joining four naked people she had never seen before. In yet another typical scenario, two blocks away from the centre of the mounting traffic jam, Patricia Parker was leaning against the picket fence of the taco shop.

"Street theatre is such a wonderful thing," she said to her friend Allison who had arrived with their takeout order.

"Awesome," agreed Allison. "This boring old town has suddenly sprouted good vibrations."

"No doubt to do with these," Patricia offered her the bag of Moodatoms. "Did you try the blue ones? Oh my hit the sky never coming back and that's no lie." Patricia popped one in her mouth and offered the bag to Allison.

"We're outta the blue, there's a red one for you."

For no explainable reason everything Patricia was about to say turned into a rhyme.

"Where did you get the blues?"

"There was easy access to a free sample booth earlier, but now the lineup is stretched around the block."

"Do you want to hang around here or jump into the action."

"Let's finish our tacos and then dive in."

They scoffed the tacos quickly and headed for the pool of bodies clambering over one another near the town hall. This is one hot city!! Spring Break for adults. An event that could possibly turn into a national holiday. Bacchanalia across the planet! On every main street, in every downtown. But right here and now in this usually orderly community the traffic was at a standstill. Cars parked in haphazard fashion. People abandoning their vehicles and climbing into the cars of complete strangers and then moving on to the next. Arnold Costa was trying to grasp what the heck was happening in his familiar territory. Heads, bodies, legs at random angles sticking out of the car windows and the doors. An orchestra of moans and giggles filtered through the summer evening building to a crescendo. Helicopters overhead scanning the activities below. X-Ray binoculars trained on the houses and apartments of the city. Doors left wide open to invite partygoers for the wall-to-wall screenings on instant replay.

* * *

Molly looked at the stranger again. He was quite good looking. No question she was feeling aroused and if Arnold was having a good time, why shouldn't she? He would never arrive in time to save the ducks anyway, not at the rate they were being knocked over. She looked at the hand Oliver had placed on her leg and decided if it would save a duckling or two, it would be worth it. She stared at the changing lights in the sky pulsating over the city skyline. Closing her eyes Molly felt a wave take hold, lifting her upwards towards its centre, rolling like mercury spiraling, before exploding into the brightest fireworks display she had ever seen. Transforming night into day, day into night and then back again. Molly opened her eyes to a beautiful warm sunny evening. She still saw the cars snaking their way to and from the city. The man was gone. The park was alive with the voices of families and children. Molly sat there in amazement trying to make sense of what had transpired. Where was Arnold? She looked up and there he was. Arnold walking along the path towards by a row of ducks behind him.

"Sorry I'm late," he said. "Big event downtown. Got held up in the traffic. I've brought some friends along to say hello."

The ducks waddled to the edge of the pond then plopped into the water, clucking all the way. Molly smiled and embraced her hero.

* * *

Sydney, Australia. Oliver Black looked down from the top of the revolving restaurant. He was really enjoying his visit here. A young vibrant city embracing a good time lifestyle. Perfect for the product he was peddling. He took the Pez dispenser out of his pocket placed two large silver capsules on the tip of his tongue and lined up two pigeons roosting on the balustrade. He took aim. PPPPRRRREEEEP. PPPRRRRREEEEPP. The birds fell in a nose dive but transformed into giant translucent butterflies before they hit the pavement. As they fluttered away, a beautiful woman standing nearby, witnessed this. She looked at him in astonishment and smiled. Oliver smiled back at her. He offered the bag from his pocket to the woman.

"An amazing product."

"What are they?'

"Moodatoms. They are a safe mood enhancement product. You choose. A change of scenery, mind, heart or mood. Try one. Free samples this weekend only. Then we're off to Europe. Choose any colour capsule that appeals to you. You will understand the future of pleasure."

"What about the silver ones."

"Ahh. The Silveratoms. Not recommended for first timers. However, they will be available in the very near future. Guaranteed by Orwellian Pharmaceuticals to deliver a life changing promise."

"Life changing?"

"Standard Moodatoms give you experience of choosing pleasure. With Silveratoms, you will experience the ability to rearrange the design of this world beyond your wildest dreams. You will be an avatar. An architect for the future of our planet and the people who live here. With the ability to control the five elements and given the ultimate gift. The pleasure of power."

(10)
ADONIS MAKES A COMEBACK

Adonis was having a tantrum. Not that there was anything unusual about that. He was running up and down the stairs of his walk-in closet searching for his favourite toupee. The closet served as a museum of his cherished memories and he would often spend hours on end there, lost among reflections of past stardom. Those glorious days of the nineties, when as leader of *Adonis and The Trashcans*, he had rocked around the world. A leader of a super group, that sold a ton of product, download videos and c.d's. And lasted about all of fifteen minutes. However, a super group nonetheless. Now, Adonis was rummaging through crap-loads of this memorabilia, gathering dust in boxes.

"Holy Zeus, whatever did I do with that head rug. It cost me a fortune."

Old photos, tee shirts, baseball caps, gold records that had served as coke plates. A number of rock star singing dolls made in his likeness. A box of melted bubble gum chews with his face on the wrapper. Costumes and outfits in every color imaginable, mostly constructed from industrial plastic garbage bags combined with leather strips and silver studs and fashioned by a top designer whose name was long forgotten. This was 2031 and Adonis looked older than Keith Richards ever could have. Catching his reflection in a discarded hub cap ashtray he began pursing his lips, once recognised and adored as his sexy pout. What had brought about this facial contortion making him look like a constipated bulldog? Out of the blue, he had received an offer nobody should have made but he couldn't refuse. He was endeavouring to look his most appealing for a purpose. And everything depended on the Face Time call he was about to place. Now, on the comeback trail, it was imperative Adonis convince his drummer Porgy Lark to re-enlist. They had been on bad terms ever since Adonis stiffed Porgy out of his last royalty share payout and Adonis knew, Porgy was no pushover when fighting for his fair share. This had been clearly demonstrated when he had ripped the hair piece off the head of Adonis on public television. Chasing him through the corridors of the broadcast studios and onto the streets of Istanbul, waving "the sword of death," an inch from his neck. This deadly weapon was said to be the authorised replica of the instrument Attila the Hun used when severing a thousand heads from their bodies, to secure his reign of terror. Porgy had purchased this legendary blade at a pawn shop on their tour of Egypt, never realizing at the time they were churning out this 'authentic' heirloom in the parking lot at the back of the very same shop. They sold at least a dozen replicas every day. In fact, he passed a guy pushing a cart with that same item on sale at half the price five minutes after he'd left the shop, clutching his prize purchase. It should be said, Porgy was never the brightest candle on the cake. The show they did that night was the last time they had played together. And that final photo of Adonis, in abject terror, with his bald head and a few strands of hair sticking out like a worn scouring pad, being chased by Porgy, did not enhance future marketing potential. The band broke up soon afterwards and returned home, which translated as having their mom cook, wash, and clean up after them. That was also the last time Adonis had seen his name and picture on any front page. He went so far underground, no one even bothered looking for him. Living like a recluse, no longer in the spotlight, Adonis had taken to wearing pull-on hair pieces even when grocery shopping. Utilising chenille cleaning mitts, made of one hundred percent polyester micro fibre, for that purpose. Available at the Dollar Emporium, machine washable and in a number of bright colours. The price was right.

But that wasn't what he was looking to wear for this important call. The toupee he sought was made of human hair and had cost him a bundle. In fact, he still owed Kojo's Hair Design $6,245 for past services rendered. Now stumbling over buried mementos and discovering forgotten treasures, Adonis found his attention and purpose distracted and frustrated. He kept bumping into his better days. Which meant lingering over every item and recalling details of that occasion. He made a promise to himself. Once this reunion tour was over. Mirrors needed to be installed. On every floor in every room of the house. Thoughts of excess vanity could be easily justified. Consider it well deserved, as a present to himself, from his fans. He also considered having a giant graffiti mural of himself, painted on the outside of the house and petitioning for a neighbourhood street to be named after him. Installing video wallpaper of tour gigs and television shows, constantly playing on every wall of every room. And mirrors. More mirrors! Who could argue against it? Adonis loved Adonis and lived in complete accord with a motto he made as clear as H2O. You can never have too much of yourself when you love yourself, as much as he did. Not only would mirrors multiply various angles and reflections of your *moi*. Every room would then expand this simple fact. True legends never die! So that was settled and all well and good, but what was he doing on his hands and knees, searching under the couch? Right, the toupee. Where was that fabulous toupee?

"Ahh, Ha! There you are."

He pulled the ratty remnants from under the skirting and shook it vigorously. It had been on the losing end of many skirmishes with Skull, the mean tempered house cat, who toyed with it like a not quite dead mouse. Venting out feline frustrations for the crappy food Adonis occasionally fed him. This once immaculate human hair piece looked like a clod of wet weeds. Sticking the toupee on his head, Adonis checked out his image and hesitated.

"Hmmm; something is a little different from the last time I wore you. Wouldn't you agree. But we haven't got time to get picky about minor flaws, now have we?"

He was in the habit of talking to the toupee. As if the hairs were still alive and could talk back. And, if the hair piece could have engaged in that conversation, it would have told Adonis that the toupee was on back to front. Oh, but never mind. There was nothing unusual about that either. Okay, not quite camera ready but more importantly, it was time to make that call.

Adonis picked up the video phone and punched in the number, VAN CIRC XO5. Waiting for the signal to connect him, he caught his reflection in the chrome receiver.

"Mmmmm. Looking good. You've still got it kid. Yes, indeed. Yes, you have," he murmured…

"You called?" interrupted the image of the Bot on the other end.

"I most certainly did otherwise what are you doing here?" said Adonis preening his profile, while rearranging the rogue strands of his toupee.

"Station connection requested," droned the voice. Operator requests identification. Please verify. Press face and scan to proceed."

Adonis pressed his face against the screen and pressed scan. Zap. The operator of the west coast centre clicked into view.

"Name and verification required of person calling."

"You recognize me of course. It's me, Adonis Androgynous, you sweet thang," drawled Adonis seductively. The bot handling the connection didn't give a monkey's butt.

"Your purchasing credit community card number is showing red. Debt. Overdue 704," said the cold face indifferently. "Are you requesting to reverse charges?"

Not to be deterred Adonis broke into a golden oldie.

"Cool, just put me through, 'cos even though I'm overdue, Baby, I depend on you,"

Adonis sang to the robot on the screen. The bot proceeded. Reverse charge requested. LINKVANCOUVER TORONTOGOAHEAD CIRC XO5 READY. Adonis pressed the maxi HD colour option enhancer and waited.

"Eh. Who is it?" came the sleepy voice along with the scrambled picture on the other end.

"Vancouver. Verification accepted you're connected, go ahead."

"Porgy you ole hound dog. It's me, baby, me, Adonis?"

The silence bristled, on the other end until, "Oh sure, I remember," said the distorted image.

"Well, Baby, what have you got to say?" said Adonis, squeezing three drops of Clearviz into each eye. "calling you long distance...Me Adonis." The irresistible urge to sing once again overpowered him.

"Don't you hear me/ Don't you see me/ Don't you want me/ Don't you feel me."

The image of the squat barrel-chested guy, snorting a line of coke, came into focus. Adonis finished the song and ignoring the fact, he was being ignored, checked back into the conversation. "Hey, Porgy. We got a job to do...Me you and the Trash Cans. Nuke the doldrums and get out the sticks and brushes. Sweep out the old, get with the news."

Porgy yawned and scratched his behind. “Do you have any idea what day and year this is?”

“It’s August,” said Adonis impatiently. “August twenty third.”

“That’s right,” said Porgy. “Exactly 123 days to go before we hit 2032. We washed up twenty years ago. Remember!? Are you wasted?”

“Wait a minute. This is Adonis you’re talking to. Me, Adonis. Ice your jets and slow the boat, baby.and listen. Can you spell resurrection?”

Porgy began slowly doing so, one letter at a time. “R…E…S.U…”

“Never mind that now, Porgy. They want us. Didn’t I tell you this would happen. Didn’t I? They’re craving our reunion.”

Porgy was not convinced.

“Who is doing the craving. That ball busting lawyer of yours? Melanie suing for alimony owed?”

“No, it’s Vegas, Baby, VeeeGGUUUUSS wants us and nobody else will do.”

Porgy slumped back on the bed and lit a Marlboro.

“Vegas has been in the boneyard longer than we have. It’s a once was wonderland.”

Adonis, brushed that comment aside and began arranging strands on the retrieved toupee. “You gotta check out some of my new hair piece collection. I’m also thinking of consulting Moe and Rodriguez to design new stage togs. Hey, and remember this one Porgy?" Adonis began to sing without restraint.

It's a satellite summer / and you're feeling life's a bummer / And you wonder who will rescue you / The Trash Cans / The Trash Cans / Adonis and The Trash Cans! The Trash Cans and Adonis, That's who! Nine million copies, triple platinum. We cleaned up a pair of Jakky Awards each. Porgy...You've still got yours?"

"Sold 'em," Porgy said blowing his nose on a discarded sock."YOOOODUUUUUUNWHHHHAAAAAATTTT!?" Adonis roared.

"Yep. I sold mine to that Mexican General as an ornament for his mother's grave. We met him at that crazy restaurant. The Water Bed Bistro in the old part of LA. All you can eat burgers and hookers remember?"

Adonis, mortified by the news quickly replaced his sulky facial reaction with a more suitable cool hip demeanor. It was disturbing to even think he was getting older. Reaching for the always present vaporizer for revival and skin refreshment, he sprayed himself liberally.

"Oh, yes, indeed I do. Hot times in the city."

"Anyway, I can't see doing this gig or any other one for that matter," said Porgy interrupting Adonis spritzing himself.

"BBBbbuuuuuuttt it's a four-week gig, three million and a half green ones. A major haul of moolah. Guaranteed half a mil each plus a likely bonus for you."

"Would that 'likely' bonus also include the additional ten thousand plus you stiffed me for last time we played?"

"*Naturellement*," said Adonis. "That's not the reason I called. Who cares about money. I miss our good times together."

"Hmmm," said Porgy ever skeptical but a little more interested. "Where is this event taking place and when?"

"The Vulture Crypt on The Strip. Spring Break," said Adonis dangling the bait.

"You're outta your temple, Adonis," Porgy groaned, distributing his toxic breath through the network. "That dump had dead bodies stowed in the walls when they bulldozed it."

Adonis felt he couldn't afford losing a bad drummer because a good one would cost a fortune.

"Now, Porgy, don't let those blues throw you off a bag of gold. This is Adonis talking, remember?

Where have you been these past twenty years? The whole Vegas zone has been restored to grandiose splendour. Like an old wedding dress upgraded for a new ceremony. Reborn as an historic site. A fly paper coated with honey to attract tourists. A new Babylon mecca and..." Porgy yawned as Adonis continued, "and get this, they are having a gala reunion for the hordes of pill poppers and the junkies that once fell at our feet. Don't you remember those days, Baby? You stood eleven feet tall on those drums. Porgy, you were magggniffficent." Adonis was burbling with enthusiasm. Porgy meanwhile toddled to the fridge and opened a new six pack. He'd heard and seen it all many times before. However, there was nothing that could discourage Adonis. He was preparing for takeoff on a spiral of self-ecstasy. Overwhelmed by an irresistible surge of inspiration, recalling yet another golden oldie. Falling to the floor, Adonis stared up into the mirrored ceiling above and let loose,

"Kooler Than a Koolerator/ Hotter Than A Fire/ Baby You're my Stimulator/ Burning with Desire."

The fuel of his ego was driving him like a snake, moving on his back across the tattered bamboo mat. Oblivious to the splinters sticking into his butt and also unaware of the video phone's ten second termination warning. SHHHCRREEEP.

"Termination imminent, press surcharge button eight and then star to continue," said the voice of the boterator.

Realizing he was about to lose his audience, Adonis leapt to his feet and smacked the surcharge button, followed by the star, blitzing the operator from the screen. The image of Porgy re-emerged, slurping down a fresh Budweiser, while flicking through an old *Penthouse* magazine.

"So, Baby. Whaddya say. Do we go do this beautiful thing?"

"Hmmm. Five thousand extra per gig for me as leader of the band guaranteed, and we go," said Porgy.

"Absolutely guaranteed you get five thousand extra for each and every gig. Plus; you track the beat for the greatest act ever to come out of the nineties. Whomever might have forgotten Adonis and The Trash Cans is going to get hit with a tidal wave of revival voltage. We were voodoo then and we're coming back even bbbiiiiiggggeerrrr. Capisci!? And Porgy, keep this filed under shut up! And listen carefully, I've been writing a new song that is gonna set the media music streams on fire. The magic touch is back." Adonis could see Porgy beginning to warm up on the end tapping on the empty beer cans.

"Maybe we should make it a rock death metal love song, Boss. What's the title?"

"Chilesaurus."

"Chilesaurus. What is Chilesaurus?"

"The Chilesauras was once king. Before a space rock collided with the Earth 66 million years ago and wiped it out. The Chilesaurus is the missing link on the dinosaur family tree."

"Don't you think they might compare that dinosaur with us?"

"That's the point!"

"Uhhmm."

"The fossil they examined links it to the birds of today. We're gonna be flying again."

"Maybe I'm missing something here."

"It had a brain the size of a walnut Porgy, so you could well be right.. The Chilesaurus only ate plants. They were vegetarians."

With a paycheque in the offing, Porgy strived to be agreeable.

"Ohhhh. Uhhhhmmm. Awesome? Wow! I think you're onto something, definitely maybe."

"Obviously. We will attract a whole new fan base. Quinoa burger, seed freaks, organic coconut carrot consumers. Lettuce munchers. All chanting the lyrics to our monster comeback hit."

"Can you give me a couple of bars, Boss?"

Adonis never needed much encouragement, when asked to demonstrate his skill for the trite and humdrum. He launched into the lyrics,

"We're like the Chilesaurus. No one came before us. We're back, you can't ignore us. We're Chili Chili. Hot. Hot. We're Chilesaurus Hot. Ouch!"

"Wow, Boss. Ouch is right. I get it. Spectacular. Brilliant as always. Like old times."

"You got it. And we should spice the track, Acid Jungle Trance. Gangsta. Porn, Hardcore horror punk. Science techno disco grunge. Throw it all in there. Swedish house mafia. Rodeo all options. Grunge it into a murder ballad. Disjoint it. Then Trash it!

"It sounds pretty trashed already, or maybe I'm a little confused."

"The culture is meant to be confused. That's how it works. First you inspire the fire. Then you con 'em with the fusion. And picture this phantasmagorical staging. You and the boys will get wheeled on inside industrial apocalyptic dumpsters and climb out of them dressed in psychedelic paper bag overalls and then start ripping them to shreds as I slowly descend from the ceiling flapping ripped black angel wings. Cross-pollinating heaven and earth. Fashion for homeless people Can you dig it?"

"Got it, Boss. I will contact the boys and get them ready for rehearsal. You get back to me when the contracts are ready."

"Okay. Ciao for now."

"Ciao."

Porgy went on a search in his basement for drumsticks. Adonis knew Porgy had bought the ticket. He watched Porgy rapidly shrink into a green dot. SCHEEEUUNNKK.

"Call completed to Toronto, time: 4 min 12 sec, charge 72, we're disconnecting."

Adonis plunged the off button.

"Blast off, Baby. Vazoom and bye-bye."

Connection terminated. The black video screen stared back at him. It had no comment to make to the old man desperately trying to avert the curtains closing on his life and times of past glory. Adonis began running his fingers through the hairs of his worn backwards, ratty toupee. Checking the ghosted reflection of himself in the silent screen Adonis had a brilliant idea. His comeback tour and album would be called, "Just Like Dorian Gray."

"Hmmmm. You've always had it kid and you always will."

(11)
THE INEVITABLE REAPER

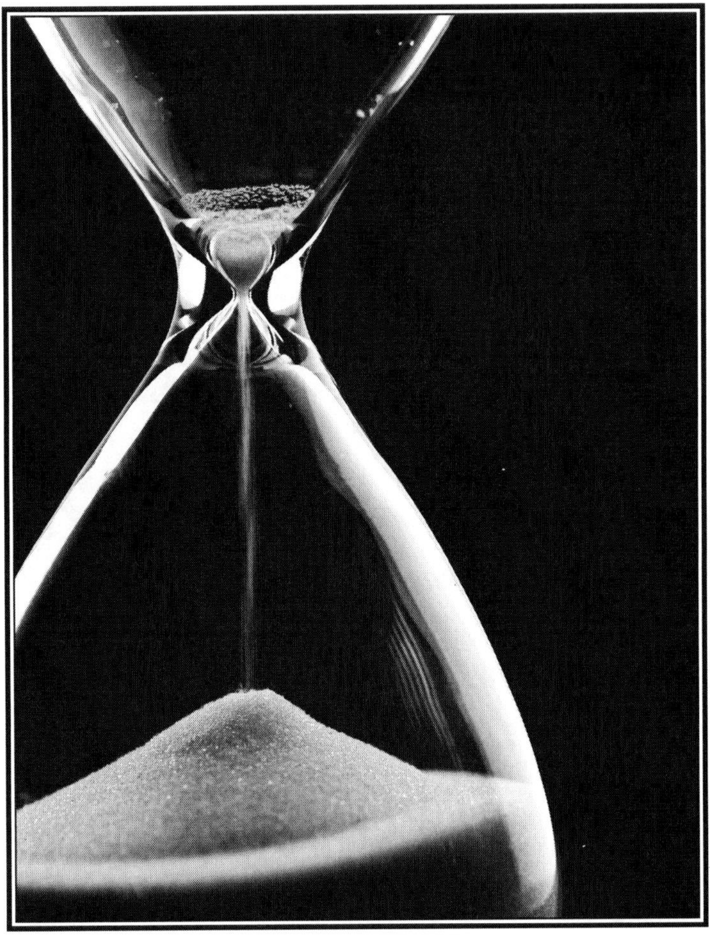

Last Year sat at the bar.

He was trying to figure some way out of the situation. Time was up. Well, time was almost up. There was always the off chance one could be granted an extension. Although, to the best of his knowledge, there was nothing on record of that ever having happened. Maybe if I'd been a leap year, he pondered. Anyhow, he wasn't and the clock was ticking away. He stared at the tall, dark, shrouded figure of the bartender wiping glasses behind the bar. Last Year applied as much charm as he could muster under the circumstances. He leaned forward trying to catch the name tag on the bartender's immaculate jacket. 'Angelo Harvester'. It rang a bell but not clearly.

"Excuse me …Angelo, …have we met before? You look somewhat familiar".

"We may have sir. I'm always hired to do this event once a year. Same time. Same place."

"Angelo Harvester. That's a very unusual name you have."

"It has quite a history let me tell you."

"I'm sure it does. I have a question for you."

"Would you like one last drink?"

"That isn't my question."

"It's your time to squander however you wish. What's your question?"

"What happens if I pretend to be another year?" Angelo indicated the giant hour glass sitting on the counter. The final grains.

"You have a few minutes. If that's enough time to be another year, go for it. And before you try pulling a fast one, next year is out of the question because that has already been assigned."

"Hmm. Let me think. What year would I like to be?"

"There isn't much time to think. I have a schedule to meet. We're in countdown right now."

"Hard to believe my innings are almost over."

Angelo Harvester smiled. "Fraid so, that's the way it goes." Last Year was persistent in playing for time.

"Still, it seems like only yesterday."

Angelo shrugged, tossed an orange in the air and expertly sliced its descent into halves, quarters and then slices with a razorsharp sickle.

"They all say that," retorted Angelo, matter of factly. "Without exception. They all say that."

"Well, if you don't mind me saying so, I don't consider myself one of those altogether ordinary years without special merit as so many of my predecessors have turned out to be. I did have my moments."

"They all say that too. It really doesn't make any difference at this point."

Angelo inserted two green Spanish Queen olives, in the eye slots of his crystal skull tip jar. And then pulled a long razor thin scythe from behind the bar. He began spitting on the blade and polishing it.

"There. Like a mirror. That's much better. Which do you prefer. The scythe or the sickle?

"They both look very dangerous."

"Not when handled with expertise. I've been master of both for as long as I can remember. But I must say i'm curious, if you could be another year, what year would you choose to be? It can be any time from the past you want. Even long before you were born. But you'd better hurry, you have less than two minutes"

"Let me be 1982. I wanna be 1982!. That was a pretty eventful time. A stand out, in fact."

"Really, why do you say that?"

Last Year was grasping at less than the final straw, desperately justifying his choice.

"Okay 1982. Take my January for instance. You must admit I made a formidable entry. Cold Sunday was a meteorological event that took place on January 17 when unprecedentedly cold air swept down from Canada and temperatures plunged across much of the United States, far below the existing record lows. Followed by a breathtaking hurricane off the coast of Barbados, a coffee shortage in Brazil, and earth shaking Richter scale tremors in Mumbai. The war in south east Asia. Assassination attempts in Rome and Venezuela. Four new revolutions in Africa. A successful overthrow of the government in Kenya. Then Argentina invaded the Falklands. And I capped it off, pardon the pun, when seven people in the Chicago area died after ingesting capsules for relieving headaches, laced with potassium cyanide. That changed the whole system of packaging pharmaceuticals forever. Not bad for starters, and memorable by any standards, wouldn't you agree. And that's just in January?"

"ACCHHOOO!" Angelo sneezed loudly. "As I recall, it was unexceptional and I missed most of it because I had a very bad cold."

"Oh right. Yes. I almost forgot about that nasty flu. That was a corker I cooked up. Started in January and lingered on for months. My February was no slouch either," continued 1982. "The virus I whipped up in Bangkok and passed around the world in twenty three days was a real doozy. Knocked them on their backsides in Moscow, Singapore, Copenhagen, Manchester, Toronto and Japan. Did you know that fifty per cent of the workers in Osaka spent three whole weeks lying on their backs watching *Cheers* on television because of it.? What a ratings booster that was. And one of the most successful plagues to hit the planet in centuries."

"If you wanted to be celebrated for a successful plague, you should have chosen 1416. Now that was a real winner," said Angelo reverently.

"Hah!" scoffed Last Year, "Fourteen sixteen was about hordes of rats and filthy sewers and is *SO* old hat. Nineteeneightytwo was where it's at."

Angelo nodded patiently. He was tired of playing nice.

"You are all the same. You know that? Such a bunch of smart arses. Blowhards, know-it-all's and hysterical show-offs when you start out of the gate. Then come December when you begin to fizzle out, it's a different story."

Last Year, doing his best to be 1982, was offended.

"As I recall, you were not this rude and impatient when we began this conversation. Maybe you should think about a change of career."

"If only I could," replied Angelo, "Barely have time to grow a decent beard before the next one of you idiots shows up. And speaking of which, it's pretty well near time up for you."

He picked up the scythe and wiped the blade on the sleeve of his bartender jacket. The reflection glinting in the overhead light.

What's it to be. the scythe or the sickle?"

"That's not fair. You didn't let me reminisce about being March, April or May. The fragrant blossoms and flowers filling the air. Lambs frolicking in the meadows. Young lovers walking along the river bank. And what about the music? *I Love Rock n' Roll* by Joan Jett. Do you remember that one? Also, I'm the year they released *Thriller* by Michael Jackson. The biggest selling album *EVAH!*. 1982. Surely that must count for something?" Angelo was having none of it.

"First of all, you were never 1982. You are *SO l*ast year. And, if I was naming my own personal favourite track for 1982, it would be *I Can't Go For That (No Can Do)* by Hall and Oates. Therefore, this game of wishing you were some other time isn't going to work for much longer because, as you can clearly see, looking at the dwindling grains of sand, you've had your time, and we need to end this charade you insisted on playing."

"Hold the clock for a bit. I haven't finished yet. Where were we…Ah yes, the remainder of nineteen eighty two. A beautiful June. Hot July. A sweltering August. The changing leaves that made for a romantic September. And the autumn winds heralding October. Halloween. And…ahhh…the crisp early frost of a misty morning in November. The first flakes." Angelo Harvester yawned and held up his hand.

"Okay. Enough. Stop right now. If there was another minute to waste I would apologize for cutting you off like this, but it's going to be a busy night. And, as I recollect nothing much of note happened in December of the year you were or wish you had been. Same old hyperbole leading up to the same old celebration. Plastic junk for presents, fake fir trees, tinsel, that ridiculous fat old imposter dressed in red with a cotton wool beard. Ho-ho-hoing in everybody's ear. A waste of time and money. Now, let's get on with the real business at hand. Final words?"

"Give me your name again. I'm gonna report you to the front desk. You can't talk about Santa Claus that way. He is beloved by millions of kids all over the world"

"Santa Fraud, more like it. That phoney overrated robber baron. And since you ask, most people that know me, know me by my nickname, The Reaper."

"You could show a little more compassion."

"And you have to understand this is a very stressful job."

"At least it's ongoing and steady work."

"You got that right."

Reaper pulled the scythe from his scabbard, ran his finger along the edge of the blade and with ever increasing speed began executing a criss-cross motion through the air.

"Ahhmm. What are you doing?"

"I'm practicing a few aerodynamic moves making sure we get a good *hasuji* when we dispatch you. Known in Japanese as *tachikaze* or sword wind. We need it to make a sharp whistle sound rather than a flat whoosh."

"Whistle or whoosh, what difference does that make?"

"Not much to you, but I'm after hearing the Aeolian tones."

"The what?"

"Aeolian tones. Aeolus was the Greek ruler of the winds." Angelo rubbed his hands and lifted the scythe. "Okay, ready?"

"Don't you have *anything* to say to me before we say goodbye?"

"Sure. I got a question for you. Who was *Time's* Man of The Year in 1982?"

"Oh, I know his name. I know it. It's on the tip of my tongue."

"Well, unfortunately you don't even have time to Google it. And it wasn't a living person. The winner of *Times* 'Man of The Year' in 1982 was the computer."

"I knew that. I knew that! Hold on while I catch my breath."

"Sure, you've got exactly ten seconds. Ten, nine, eight, seven, six, five, four…"

A loud, urgent banging on the outside door drowned out Angelo's voice as he counted down the final seconds of the past year,

"Three, two…And ONE!"

A high frequency whistle was heard as the scythe came swooping down. Last Year was severed, diced, extinguished and swept under the carpet. Simultaneously, a svelte, sensational looking figure burst through the door, dragging a bunch of well-wishers, party animals and soon-to-become, broken resolutions, along with them.

"Ta-Tah!" the brightly dressed newcomer hollered. "Everyone, check their smart phone. Happy New Year!!" Angelo Harvester wiped the blade of the scythe clean before putting it back behind the bar, then after deftly slicing a few limes and lemons with his sickle, he filled up the olive jar and turned to face the incoming new year horde thinking to himself.

"Oh, Lawdy. Here we go again. I hope this one turns out to be more rewarding than the last ten thousand did." Smiling at the cluster of bodies, clamouring eagerly at the bar, their shiny faces full of unlikely dreams and expectations, he asked;

"Now, what can I get for you punks and princesses?"

ABOUT THE AUTHOR

David Charles Simmonds

David has worked in theatre, film, and music as an actor, director, and writer. He trained and performed under contract, with the Actor's Workshop in Vancouver through the mid-seventies. He later established, owned and operated the Screen Actor's Studio in Victoria B.C. from 1985 - 2015. A founding board member of CineVic, the Society for Independent Filmmakers and the Victoria Film Festival. He has written lyrics for songs recorded by Michael Buble, Lee Greenwood, B.T.O. and others. A script writer for full length, short film and animation projects, David is currently in pre-production of one of his original plays. He is very much looking forward in the near future to meeting readers of 'The Teleporter's Handbook.'

A portion of proceeds of this book will be donated to: 'It Gets Better Canada'. A non-profit society in support of the LGBTQ Community.